Zap the Wizard and the Land of Odd

Gilly Wilkinson

For Jean & Mike

Thank you for the bed spread
& Duvet/curtains (doh!)

Happy Reading

lotsa love

Gilly X .

TAVERNER PUBLICATIONS

© Gilly Wilkinson 2002

First Published 2005

ISBN 1 901470 09 1

© 1989 GOSHCC Registered Charity Number 235825
A royalty of 50p is given to GOSHCC for every copy sold

Published by
TAVERNER PUBLICATIONS
Taverner House, Harling Road
East Harling, Norfolk

Printed by Postprint, East Harling, Norfolk

For Florran and all her friends.

Thanks to Serena, Jay and Steve, Michael,
Angela, Maggie and Mike, Jennie,
Ken and Julia, Harold and Enid, David
and to you for buying this book.

Chapter One

Peanut had endured a difficult day at school. Despite doing very well in her lessons, or possibly because of it, she had been severely bullied. Back home in the quiet sanctity of her little room, she looked at herself in the mirror. It was true. Her straggly hair did resemble a slightly shorn mop head. At ten years young she had a total of 104 freckles and two sticky-out front teeth. Black heavy rimmed spectacles framed her eyes. You can imagine the teasing she went through!

Her name didn't really help matters either. Imagine being called Peanut while being so tiny! However, Peanut did not consider this to be unusual. She didn't actually think about it at all as she stared at the mirror. She was just counting the freckles to see if any more had appeared (they seemed to move in on any patch of clear skin at their own convenience).

Peanut's parents, Mr Oliver and Mrs Ida Fatness were really quite ashamed of their daughter. She looked nothing like them. Ida was a tallish round lady who got rounder every day. All day long she gorged herself on chocolate bars, cream doughnuts, jam fingers and anything else which could be fattening. She hated to be interrupted while eating (which was nearly all the time).

Ida was having her hair done in town. She did not care that others stared at her as she persistently pushed cream buns into her mouth. She lined up ten éclairs around the sink basin, while her hair was washed. She managed to stuff nine of the long cakes, oozing cream, into her mouth. Then, just as the stylist was putting rollers into her hair, Ida began to scream:

"Thief thief, give me back my éclair." I had ten, I have only eaten nine, where is it?"

Everybody in the hairdressers stared at Ida. She had a large blob of cream on her fat nose and had gone quite purple in the face. It was then that the hairdresser realised that instead of picking up a roller, she had accidentally taken an éclair to wrap Ida's hair around. The missing éclair was at that moment sat fairly and squarely in the middle of Ida's head, delicately wound in hair! Of course, this was all sorted out and explained away as being the greatest rage and Ida believed herself to be at the height of fashion. Once the rollers had been removed Ida left the salon with the éclair neatly entwined in her new fluffy hairdo, simply simpering with pride at the innovation of saving one's treat for later.

I am afraid that when Ida returned home, Peanut just stared and then, much to her horror, let out an unusually loud snort. She didn't mean to, she knew that it could only bring trouble, but the fact remained that the harder she had tried not to laugh, the larger the laugh seemed to get. It started in her tummy and grew louder and louder as it climbed to her mouth to be confined no longer. Escaping in a loud snort, then hastily, badly disguised as a sneeze.

"What was that?" yelled Ida Fatness.

"A sneeze, Mummy" replied an apologetic Peanut, gripping her hands together in front of her.

"A sneeze was it? I'll give you sneeze!" Peanut was sent to bed, without any tea. This was quite the worst punishment that Ida could think of, loving food so greatly herself. But… it was no punishment at all to Peanut who barely ate enough to feed a fly. Indeed, it was almost a reward. Peanut could use the time for her favourite hobby – reading!

All her pocket money was spent on books. She seldom bought sweets because that was all she was given to eat at home.

Peanut's bedroom was almost filled with books. The room wasn't very big and there was scarcely enough room for her small bed, but that was the way she liked it.

There were books about horses and lions and tigers. Books for hobbies and crafts. Big books, small books and, oh, so many I cannot begin to mention them all. What luck to be allowed to sit and read quietly for the rest of the evening.

Of course, her father may say differently upon his return. You never can tell with parents can you? But for the moment, Peanut settled down with her edition of *'Zap the Wizard and the Land of Odd.'*

Downstairs, Ida had opened the enormous fridge to look for something nice to prepare for Oliver's dinner. In doing so she had noticed a lovely creamy chocolate fudge cake which was sitting invitingly untouched, on a foil gateau platter.

It was more than fifteen minutes since she had last eaten, so Ida decided to have a slice while preparing the cream of tomato soup, followed by bangers and mash with chips and a dessert of apple pie, vanilla and strawberry ice-cream and chocolate sauce. This was to be followed by cheese and biscuits, after-dinner mints and a small 7lb turkey for supper.

Ida cut a tiny sliver of the cake and put it onto a plate, which she covered with stretch cellophane and put into the fridge, while picking up the rest of the cake in one hand and stuffing it, unceremoniously, into her mouth. Chocolate flakes fell to the floor and fudge oozed through her fat fingers. She turned the radio on and began making dinner.

Oliver Fatness worked at the bank as the Assistant to the Manager's Assistant. He was very proud of his job and could often be heard boasting how he could run the bank 'single handed' and how he was 'indispensable' to them. That they didn't know how 'lucky they were'. Oliver was a bald man, even rounder and fatter than Ida, (which is hard to imagine) but he had a very bad temper. In fact nobody at the bank liked him very much. They were not too polite to say so; they were just petrified of being rolled over and flattened by Oliver.

Every morning Oliver squeezed himself into an ever-tightening pinstripe suit, rasping and wheezing as he tried to catch his breath. He complained loudly about his 'stupid tailor.'

After a ginormous breakfast he would get into his car and leave for work. All the staff were on their best behaviour in front of him. They worried that one day he would lose his temper – should he be so overcome with rage at being unable to find a letter in the filing cabinet in time, (which was usually three seconds) he might roll over one of them and squash them. So they worked well and diligently all day, only stopping to mutter rude things about him when he was in another room.

The Bank Manager did not like Oliver much either. He would like to sack him but couldn't in case he got squashed. And so Mr Oliver Fatness remained the Assistant to the Manager's Assistant and believing himself to be indispensable.

Oliver had just locked the bank ready to go home for the day when there was an unfortunate incident. Unfortunate that is, for Peanut…

As he climbed into his car, Oliver heard a noise similar to gunshot. BANG, BANG. Bang BANG! All four of his tyres burst. One tyre would have been a simple matter of swapping it for the spare, but all four was a calamity.

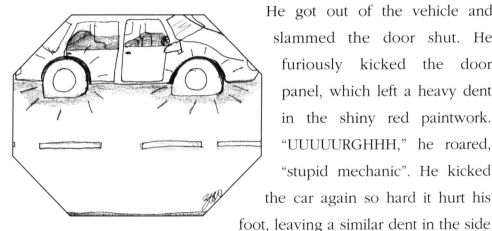

He got out of the vehicle and slammed the door shut. He furiously kicked the door panel, which left a heavy dent in the shiny red paintwork. "UUUUURGHHH," he roared, "stupid mechanic". He kicked the car again so hard it hurt his foot, leaving a similar dent in the side panel. "Uuuuurgh," he raged, going quite blue in the face. In fact he ranted and raged and roared until quite a crowd had gathered, most of whom believed there to be an escaped elephant on the rampage when first they heard the commotion.

Oliver looked up and saw all the expectant faces of the crowd staring at him. "UUUUUURGHHH," he roared at them, now quite beside himself with anger. As quickly as the crowd had gathered they now dispersed. I mean to say, you never can be too careful and nobody actually enjoys being squashed to death.

Oliver took one more look at his car and snorted. There was nothing else for it. It was late, Oliver was hungry. His sandwiches had run out a whole hour ago and he wanted his dinner. He picked up his briefcase and started to waddle towards the bus stop.

Again, unfortunately for Peanut, the bus was late and Oliver Fatness hated waiting. His anger grew bigger and bigger until finally, a whole minute and a half late, the bus drew up to a shuddering halt.

Oliver pushed his way onto the bus, knocking ladies and youngsters aside with his protruding elbows as he went. He sat and the bus slowly began to trundle onward. When the conductor came to ask for money for the fare, the poor man was greeted by a blast of nasty words one inch from his face, bellowed by a furious, tired and hungry purple-faced Oliver.

"I pay my taxes, how dare you be so late?"

The conductor cringed against the hand-rail, holding his ticket machine in front of him for protection.

"You stupid, stupid man," roared Oliver, stamping his foot.

All the passengers stuck their fingers in their ears so their eardrums wouldn't pop.

As Oliver continued to shout, the buttons on his waistcoat, which had already been at breaking point without a temper tantrum, suddenly burst forth. Zing, ping, whiz, whiz!

They shot through the air towards the passengers who ducked, fingers still firmly embedded in their earlobes. Thankfully everybody, with one exception, managed to avoid being struck by the button missiles. The exception sadly, was the bus driver who was hit neatly in the back of his neck, right upon his sleep pipe. The driver instantly fell asleep and the bus stopped right in the middle of the busy road.

Oliver was in fact rather alarmed by this. Underneath all the blustering bad temper and roaring voice, he was a coward! Deciding then and there it was time to get off the bus, he leaned down and grabbed his briefcase. I am only one road away from where I live, he reasoned. Oddly, he didn't mind the walk and the thought of impending dinner cheered him slightly. The driver slept on, a little grin playing around his mouth as he dreamed happy dreams.

Oliver pushed and heaved his way toward the exit, but oh calamity! As he turned to look at the driver, Oliver somehow became wedged. He couldn't turn around nor could he move forward or back.

"Ouch, I'm stuck, oh ow, oh dear, oooof," he said, glaring at his fellow passengers.

The passengers glared straight back. There was only one exit on this bus and with Oliver blocking it, they too were stuck!

Upon realising this fine advantage over Oliver, the conductor, more angry than worried, pulled a nasty face at him. Then imitating Oliver's voice said with a leer, "Can't you breathe in, you stupid man?"

Oliver breathed in but nothing happened, he was still very stuck. The conductor grinned in a very nasty way and said, "Breathe in some more."

Oliver did breathe in some more, going quite red with the effort. Still nothing happened. Just then a policeman came over to find out why the bus was holding up the traffic. He was not impressed to find the driver asleep. He was even less impressed to find Oliver blocking the doorway and a rabble of irate passengers. He was concerned that these people had escaped the local loony-bin, but in fact they had just forgotten to remove their fingers from their ears. They continued to shout at each other and hear absolutely nothing.

The policeman scratched his head thoughtfully. Just then, Oliver made an extraordinary noise. Turning, the officer saw Oliver had turned purple and his eyes were bulging. Grief! A heart attack, he thought, leaping into action.

"Breathe out you stupid man," shouted the conductor, realising that Oliver was still trying to breathe in to free himself.

One by one the passengers caught sight of the police officer and took their fingers from their lobes. Gradually the shouting stopped; there was an expectant silence. Then, "How are we to get off this bus?" asked a blue-coated lady.

"I wonder," said the officer rubbing his hand to and fro across his chin.

"Yes?" said Oliver, hopefully.

"Well, if all the passengers push and I pull and you breathe in," he replied, "you may be released."

Everybody thought this idea was worth trying. They took up their positions. The passengers pushed, the conductor pushed, the policeman pulled, Oliver breathed in. At first nothing seemed to happen. Then suddenly Oliver lurched forward with great force, knocking the policeman backward. Oliver continued, straight over the top of the officer. He hit the pavement outside with a loud boingggg! Bouncing once, twice and then rolling. At the same time the passengers and ticket collector all shot forward and landed upon the policeman as a mass of arms and legs.

Oliver continued down the hill and into a cluster of dustbins just outside his house, with a loud crash. Hearing the commotion, Ida dashed to the front door, only to find an open-waistcoated Oliver, sitting upon the pavement with a smelly rotten cabbage on his head. His briefcase was just visible from one of the bins.

Peanut, sitting reading on her windowsill, glanced down. Oh dear, she thought, I don't suppose Daddy will be in a very good mood now.

Daddy wasn't!

Chapter Two

Daddy was angry with everybody; his impending dinner didn't even make him feel better. When Ida told him that Peanut was in her room for being cheeky he saw an excellent vent for all his pent-up embarrassments and temper. He stomped up the stairs to her bedroom.

"You," he shouted, "are going to stay in your room for a week, do you hear?"

"Yes Daddy," said Peanut meekly, thinking this wasn't going to be so bad after all.

"You," he pointed, "will not have any breakfast, dinner or tea, do you hear?"

"Yes Daddy," replied Peanut even more meekly, wondering if he had forgotten her name.

"You," Oliver screamed, his arms waving madly, "will apologise to your mother." So saying he turned on his heels so quickly that the rotting cabbage still perched upon his head fell to the floor and rolled down the stairs. Oliver did not wait for a reply; he slammed the bedroom door and stamped down the stairs.

"Yes, Daddy," said Peanut to the closed door. She wondered: 1. How she was to apologise to her mother without leaving her bedroom. Ida certainly wouldn't climb the stairs to see her. 2. Why both her parents had taken to wearing foodstuffs on their heads, and 3. Why Daddy seemed to think she couldn't hear him despite the fact he'd been shouting. It is a strange world, she thought.

Peanut looked around her bedroom. Things aren't so bad, she told herself. After all, she had only been told not to have breakfast, dinner or tea. She had a whole basket of fruit, won for being top of English. I am allowed fruit. She smiled contentedly.

A week of reading, what a wonderful treat! Better by far than being forced to sit in the kitchen to eat one sticky item after another to "build you up." She didn't want to be built up. Taller yes, rounder no! Oliver and Ida ate enough for them all. Peanut secretly believed that one day they would burst if they continued.

Between you and I, had Peanut's parents been less obsessed with food, they might have noticed just how clever their little girl was. They could have helped her to make the best of herself with a trip to the dentist to straighten her teeth or a trip to the optician to find prettier glasses. Even a visit to the stylist to cut Peanut's hair into a softer style. But no, they did nothing, except to eat of course!

Peanut picked up her book; *'Zap the Wizard and the Land of Odd'*. She settled herself comfortably into the small window seat and started to read Chapter Three...

Zap was not at all the name of the Wizard, but in fact, an open invitation! Bean slowly reached down to pick up the shiny Super-Zapper. He carefully fitted his finger against the curve of the trigger. He squeezed and out shot a bright pink star. Zzing Ffizz. It shot across the clearing and landed splat! on the trunk of what appeared to be an upside-down tree.

Bean let out a surprised laugh then once again took aim, this time at the wall of a pudding-style white cottage. Gurgle, gurgle Zap! went the Super-Zapper and out shot a yellow moon shape. Splat! It hit the wall.

"Wow" said Bean in surprised delight.

Wow, thought Peanut. Wouldn't it be good if I had one of those? I could decorate my plain old wallpaper with stars and moons. She turned the page and continued…

You can have one! read the next page. *Why don't you come and have a go?*

Peanut looked down at the page number. "That's odd." she said. "This paragraph doesn't follow on." She turned back a page to see if any were missing. Sometimes, when you buy a secondhand book, pages are torn or have fallen out. "Number 19," she read. She turned the page, "number 20," she read. This time, the first words on page 20 read:

"Well, are you coming?"

Peanut pushed her glasses back into place on her nose and frowned. "That's odd!" she repeated. Then she removed her glasses altogether and polished them on her sleeve. The words seem to have changed, she thought. She replaced her glasses to the bridge of her nose, perplexed. Again she peered at the page:

"Look, stop being so dithery and get a wiggle on. Answer the question, are you coming or not?" read the book.

"How odd!" exclaimed Peanut. "This book is definitely strange," she declared to nobody. She began to close the book, not quite sure what to do. The hair on the back of her neck felt shivery. Then to her dismay, Peanut realised she was feeling decidedly strange. She opened, then narrowed her eyes, and had an odd sensation of falling towards the still-open book. She shut her eyes tight, sure she was about to hit the ground. One hand flew to her face to protect her glasses and…

Nothing happened. Slowly, she opened one eye. The other flew open in amazement. She was lying on a thick green carpet of mossy grass, looking up at a very tall, lanky boy. She felt confused.

"Hello!" said the boy, "I'm Bean."

"Hello," said Peanut, "I'm dreaming."

"Strange name," said Bean offering a hand up.

"Oh, no, that's not my name. I'm Peanut. You can talk," she added. Carefully she stood up.

"Strange name," said Bean with a grin.

"My name IS Peanut." she said, staring up at Bean, "and I'm either dreaming or…" she paused, "dead?"

"You look quite alive and very awake to me," said Bean.

"Yes," said Peanut, "so do you. But that is the way it happens with dreams. One minute you are being chased by a fire-breathing dragon and the next you wake up and remember that you forgot to do your maths homework. I'll wake up in a moment," she insisted.

"Okay," said Bean, "I'll give you one minute. If you haven't woken by then, we must both believe that you are already awake. Agreed?" He looked at his watch.

"Agreed," replied Peanut confidently.

"Ready, steady, go!"

Peanut closed her eyes and opened them again. Bean continued to stare at his watch. Peanut pinched herself lightly on her arm.

"Thirty seconds," said Bean. Peanut pinched herself harder – "Ow!" she cried.

"Ten seconds," said Bean.

Peanut started to jump up and down. She believed that if she really were asleep, the noise would bring her father upstairs to tell her off for making so much noise.

"Five seconds" said Bean. Nothing happened.

"Time up," cried Bean triumphantly, "I win".

"All right," said Peanut, "so where am I?"

"I think," he replied, "we are in the Land of Odd. At least, that's what the signpost says."

"You mean you don't know for certain?" Peanut looked around her.

"Not really. You see, I thought I was in the library reading a book. Then, I wasn't there at all. I was here. The book had gone, the library had vanished and I was lying by the signpost. After looking around me for a while I decided to explore a little. That's when I found this." He held up the Super-Zapper.

"Hey, that's like in my book! I was reading all about you, next thing I knew I arrived here!"

By some strange coincidence, both Bean and Peanut had been reading 'Zap the Wizard and the Land of Odd' prior to their strange arrival here.

"That explains it then," said Bean cheerfully.

"Yes, I suppose it does," said Peanut doubtfully. She glanced down at the Super-Zapper.

"Can I have a go with that?"

"If you like." Bean passed her the Zapper, which she took and examined more closely. They started to walk along the pathway. Peanut held the Zapper up to her shoulder and aimed at the nearby cottage door. Zzzzing, a bright pink star shape flew over the garden wall and landed Splat, on the door handle. Peanut shouted triumphantly, "There, I did it, I can do it, I can do it." She aimed again, then fired. Zzap! A blue triangle shot into the sky and disappeared from view. Whizz! A green moon landed splat on the garden wall.

"Careful," cried Bean, "I don't want to be zapped."

"Sorry, got carried away," she grinned sheepishly, "I wish I could have one of these back home."

Bean grinned. He thought so too. He aimed at the doorway, just below Peanut's pink star. Zzap, seven colours shot out of the Super-Zapper forming a rainbow. Red, orange, yellow, green, blue, indigo and violet. It caught the light as it flew through the air and landed across the cottage door.

"Wow!" said Peanut, "that's brilliant!" Just as Bean was about to respond, a voice asked,

"Who's that? Who's there?"

They looked at each other, then over the garden wall, Peanut looked straight into the periwinkle-blue eyes of a little old man. He had grey hair sticking out in two tufts just above each ear and was wearing a top hat and a rainbow-coloured cloak.

Chapter Three

"Sorry," said Peanut as she walked towards the gate, "we didn't know that anybody lived here."

"We?" asked the man.

"Yes," said Peanut looking around, "Bean and I, we didn't mean to cause any harm." Bean emerged sheepishly from behind the tree. He'd leapt out of his skin and immediately hidden. Once given away by a slower-thinking Peanut he decided to give himself up. "Hello," grinned a red-faced Bean, looking towards his shoes. "I'm sorry too," he added.

"Whatever for?" asked the man in surprise. He peered at them both from under shaggy grey eyebrows. "My word!" he exclaimed, "you are both real children aren't you? What a treat! Come in, come in. Come along, you are just what I need." He started off along the path toward the cottage door.

Bean turned as if to run again, but Peanut grabbed his sleeve and gave him 'a look'. They stopped at the cottage door so Peanut could see in, just in case they were in danger.

"What did he mean by 'real'?"

"Hungry, I expect," stated the man as he put the kettle on, "you got me good and proper." He chuckled, pointing to a section of rainbow paint on his hand, "Tea is the least I can do." So saying, he waved his arms in the air and a baby elephant fell straight through the kitchen table. The children walked through the doorway and into the kitchen, staring at the elephant. "Umm," said the man thoughtfully going towards the table. "Sorry," he said to the elephant, "that wasn't supposed to happen. I have a spot of bother with my cloak" as if this explained everything. The children continued to stare in disbelief.

"That's okay," said the elephant getting to his feet. He shook himself and trotted off towards the open doorway and into the garden. The children ran to the window to watch him depart, they were dumb with amazement.

Peanut turned back toward the man. "Who did you say you are?"

"I didn't say," smiled the man, "but," he added, "my name is Boris. I am certain that you have already heard of me." Then he beamed a huge grin at them, showing his wisdom teeth. "Correct me if I'm wrong, but you didn't get further than the third chapter. It's like this," he said, waving his left arm from which a frog fell, then hopped across the floor to the open doorway, "to get to the Land of Odd there are certain conditions which must be achieved. 1. You must be pleasant. 2. You must live with difficult circumstances. 3. You absolutely categorically MUST be reading *'Zap the Wizard and the Land of Odd.'* I do prefer that you *enjoy* reading it. 4. You must state 'that's odd' twice, because that is the password." Boris finished speaking and looked triumphantly around at Bean and Peanut.

They were sat hunched up, with their arms over their heads, watching a menagerie of creatures which had been appearing from somewhere below the ceiling and crashing to the floor. The whole time Boris had been speaking, he had also been waving his arms. This seemed to have a seriously bad effect on what did or did not appear in the small cottage kitchen.

"So now you know" added Boris, waiting for some response. He removed his top hat and placed it on the surface. Peanut could see that although the tufts of grey grew profusely from the sides of his head, Boris was in fact quite bald on top.

"Boris," said Peanut, "why was it that when we were entering the cottage, you said that we are real children?"

Boris looked at her closely and said, "Well, you are real aren't you?"

"Yes of course, but that's not what I meant… er do you think you could sit on your hands while you explain this time, only it gets very dangerous in here."

"Of course," Boris blushed slightly, "well, you must realise there are so many conditions to get here that it doesn't happen very often. You see, there could be a child who has been less well treated but who doesn't have the book. Or, doesn't say the password. Maybe they are not very nice. Some may have the book but not enjoy it, putting it down at chapter one or two. If it were easier to come here, there would be too many, people would notice and we would get shut down, or the wrong sort could get here and ruin it for everybody. We only have room for special children."

Bean nodded and Peanut wondered about the badly treated children who were not allowed to read or have books. Rules could be changed sometimes.

"Why are we 'just what you need'?" asked Bean, who still had his arms across the top of his head, just in case.

"There are things that real children can do, which we are unable to do by ourselves. Some of them are quite important things; others are things such as playing fun games."

"What games?" asked Bean and Peanut in unison.

"Zapping, for starters. The Super-Zappers are my invention. I have left boxes of them all over the Land of Odd. Children have to locate a Zapper then try to find me. The rules are simple, if you successfully manage to zap me you get three wishes. Plus I make you tea – when I can manage to get my cloak to operate correctly," Boris added.

"Should I prepare some tea in the normal fashion for now?" asked Peanut.

"Now there's an idea, what do you think Bean?"

"I'll help" said Bean without hesitation, "where do you store your food?"

"There's salad in the garden, bread in the bread-bin and tea in the caddy. I shall continue to try with my cloak while you are busy. I have to get it working again for other things. In fact," said Boris with a gleam in his eyes, "I'll race you!"

He bounded out of his chair, tripped over the bottom of his cloak and fell, almost crushing a snail who was still making his way towards the door. Boris apologised.

"Not at all my dear boy," drawled the snail, continuing on its way.

Peanut and Bean dashed to the cupboards and started piling food onto the work surface. Bean sped towards the door to grab some salad while Peanut buttered the bread. Boris had succeeded in making a new table appear, but stood outside to try and magic some food (so any further elephants could not destroy the new table).

Bean picked a lettuce and tomatoes then headed for the cucumber frame. Peanut stacked bread onto a plate then laid the table with a cloth, plates and cutlery. Just then Boris triumphantly re-appeared carrying a tray laden with all sorts of goodies. "There!" he stated proudly, "you have done tea, I have done dessert." He smiled, "we all win that round."

"Have you had much difficulty with your cloak?" asked Peanut as they sat at the table.

"No, not too much. I tore it walking through the woods last Funday, it simply needs a patch."

Peanut poured tea into the bright orange cups. "Why don't you mend it then, Boris. I can even sew it if you like?" She tucked into a salad sandwich.

"I would mend it myself if I could, but it's not that simple. The patch has to be a special one. Each of the stars and moons on my cloak are made of curtain material from your world. That is why it is so colourful. *That* is what gives the cloak its magic. The catch is, I cannot visit your world. I'm not grumpy or moody enough."

"I could have brought you some if you'd said," Peanut nibbled at some lettuce with all the appearance of a bespectacled mouse.

"No you couldn't," said Boris, "curtains cost money and your parents would be furious if you began cutting up your curtains. No, the material must be from the remnants only. Not many people keep them these days. Everything is ready made, off-the-peg."

"I have a bag full of remnants, I made my curtains in needlework at school. I kept the leftover material to make other things out of. Mummy didn't want them so they are my very own!"

"What are your parents like, Peanut?" asked Bean with interest.

"Daddy is usually very angry. He works in the bank and his suit doesn't fit very well. Oh, and just recently he has taken to wearing vegetables on his head. Mummy is always busy making dinner or tea or snacks. They are big and like food." She didn't mention her mother's éclair hair-clip. "What are yours like?" she asked.

Bean finished chewing his cheese sandwich, then replied "my mum is almost a giant. She's almost as tall as one. She plays sport a lot and eats at the club. My dad is even taller. They asked him if he would consider painting the bridge over the Thames, as he wouldn't need a ladder. He did it too, wearing his jogging shorts, last summer. They both love sport, but I don't."

"Ah," said the Wizard knowingly. Bean continued eating. He picked up one of the pink and blue biscuits, which Boris had conjured. Peanut was still nibbling her lettuce and tomatoes. She loved it; seldom did she get anything so refreshing to eat. Something not sticky, not sweet! She glanced over to Bean who appeared to be shrinking in his chair. He was frantically chewing on something as though his life depended upon it. At the same time, he reached over towards the plate of biscuits.

Peanut watched him avidly, trying to work out if Bean was slouching or shrinking. Both appeared to be happening, but no, he was definitely shrinking. By now, his jaws were working like pistons as he crammed one biscuit after another into his mouth.

"What are those Boris?" Peanut asked, pointing at the biscuits while remembering it to be rude to point. All the same, a very logical thing to do if you don't know the name of something!

"Ah," said Boris, "something special. We usually have them on Funday. They are wish biscuits." He glanced at Bean as he spoke, then leaning confidentially toward Peanut, he added, "Bean is wishing he can be the size of the rest of his class mates, so that is what happens. All quite simple."

"Can you wish for anything?" asked Peanut.

"Of course," nodded Boris, "but it does have to be something you really want to happen."

Peanut finished her sandwich and took one. She popped it into her mouth and chewed a little. "Wow!" she exclaimed in pleasure, "it tastes just like roast beef. I thought it would be sweet. I'm glad it's not though."

"One of mine tasted like peppermint ice-cream" said a medium-sized Bean.

Unlike him, Peanut only had a small appetite. She was feeling full to the extent that her tummy hurt slightly. But, she wanted something very badly indeed, so for once in her life she was eating despite the fact she wasn't hungry.

What Peanut wanted more than anything else in the whole wide world would be to have really clear eyesight. Previously, she had always pretended that her glasses didn't bother her, but only because there was nothing else to be done but wear them or keep bumping into things. The latter hurt too much to keep doing for long. The glasses were a nuisance. They hurt her nose and her ears. She had to be careful all the time in case they got broken. Children who were obviously glad that they weren't wearing glasses, called her nasty names. You would think that *not* wearing glasses would be gift enough, without making those who did, suffer further.

She finished chewing her biscuit with her eyes firmly shut. Then she peered at the things on the table. There were fuzzy plates and cups all swirling around before her eyes. That sinking feeling in the pit of her stomach occurred as she realised her wish hadn't come true. Momentarily she felt utterly miserable. Her eyes were even worse than before. Something had gone dreadfully wrong. "Maybe I just didn't want it badly enough," she thought, trying to focus on her plate.

Boris had been watching her. "Why don't you take your glasses off?" he asked, guessing at her wish. "If your eyes are truly better, your spectacles will make the sight worse."

Again, Peanut firmly closed her eyes. With renewed hope she pulled her glasses off. Holding her breath she opened her eyes. An amazing view was before her. The colour, the clarity, no reflections like you get with glasses. "Goodness, I really can see, I didn't know it could be like this." Climbing down from her chair, she spun around, almost toppling over in her haste to see everything. She went to the window and looked out. "Wow!" she said.

Running back to Boris, she grinned. "Thank you very much. This is wonderful, everything is so clear."

Boris smiled. "Now I think you two need somewhere to stay. You had better get ready and go to bed. We have a busy day ahead of us, Myday always is."

"Your day?" asked Bean. Is it your birthday?"

"No, 'Myday' you know, as in the days of the week. Oh, you don't know" he corrected himself. "Today is Funday. Tomorrow is Myday, the first day in the week. Then we have Yourday, Ourday, Theirday, Friendsday, Sadday and Funday." "On Myday," he explained, "everybody does things for themselves. These would be things that they like to do, hobbies or walks or listening to music. Then on Yourday, people do things specifically for you that they think you might like. Ourday is the day on which we all do things in family units, all together, such as picnics."

"That's brilliant," said Peanut, "I bet that makes a wonderful sense of community and friendship."

"School wouldn't be nearly so necessary because you can never stop learning with such great interest in things and each other," Bean remarked thoughtfully.

Boris nodded. "Theirday is when family units go and help other family units to do things that they cannot do easily on their own. Friendsday is a lovely day when you go and see all the friends that you can manage to see in one day. Sadday is not as good as other days, but into every life a little rain must fall. Children go home on Sadday. If they are going, that is the day they go. Sometimes never to return," he added, almost to himself, "anyway, it's very late and you two should have been asleep long ago."

He opened the doorway through to the stairs that they wearily climbed. Upstairs there were four doors along a dark passageway. "They are all attic rooms," Boris explained, "so you must be sure not to bump your heads on the sloping parts of the ceilings." He opened the first door. "This one will suit you Peanut. Poppy had it while she was here."

Inside was the prettiest room that Peanut had ever seen. There was a creamy white carpet, which was so thick it felt like wading through the sea as you walked across it. A little pink and cream rug sat by the bed. The bed itself was so soft and springy that Peanut bounced on it just because she could, without fear of pain from rusty springs sticking through the mattress.

On the bed there was a thick quilt encased in a rainbow patchwork quilt cover. The curtains at the windows matched the quilt. Best of all

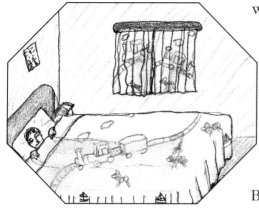

was the bookcase. It covered a whole wall, and as Peanut looked along the shelves, she discovered that she had not read even one of these books before.

"Goodnight Peanut," said Boris and Bean from the doorway. They moved along the corridor to a blue door. Boris opened it. "Bean, here you are my boy." This room also had an amazing bookcase. The carpet was pale blue and every bit as thick as the one in Peanut's room. The bed had a quilt of pale and royal blue with ships and trains chuffing and chugging around the edges of the cover.

"This is marvellous!" exclaimed Bean who had always had a grown-up style bedroom, simply because a grown-up had never consulted Bean as to what he would like. "Splendiferous, magnificently wonderful."

"I get the picture," said Boris, "you are pleased with your room. Good, thought you'd like it my boy. Now get a good rest and sleep well."

"You too," said Bean, truly meaning it. "Goodnight Boris, thank you."

Chapter Four

The next day, Peanut couldn't remember where she was. The sunshine was streaming in through the attic window and birds were singing merrily in the tree just outside. She sat up and looked all around her in disbelief until she remembered where she was. With a burst of joy and for the first time that she could ever remember, she didn't have to reach for a pair of spectacles. She no longer needed them. She sprang out of bed and hurriedly got dressed.

When she reached the kitchen she found that both Boris and Bean had beaten her to it. They were already deep in conversation.

"Good morning Peanut," beamed Boris, "would you like some breakfast?"

"Yes please," said Peanut, "could I have a slice of toast and marmalade?"

"You can have marmalade, lamalade, honey, jam, spam or sunny if you like," said Boris, "maybe you would like to try them all?"

"Just marmalade, please," said Peanut looking at the spread on the table before her. She sat down and Bean offered her a slice of toast. "Thank you," she took the proffered slice and thinly spread the marmalade on it – "what is Sunny?"

Boris pushed one of the little dishes across to her. "Try it, it's made here in the Land of Odd by our very own bees and, of course, Mother Nature. It is almost the same as your honey, but because our bees are happier, the sun is sunnier and therefore the nectar is slightly runnier and it makes you feel contented and happy when you eat it."

"Go on Peanut, try some. It is really lovely. So is the lamalade, though that is just lime flavoured marmalade and we do have that at home," said Bean.

"Oh, it feels warm as it goes down," said Peanut taking a bite, "I feel like I'm glowing from the inside."

"Good!" exclaimed Boris, "now if you wouldn't mind excusing me, I have some urgent spells to work on. I must get them exactly right, ready for tomorrow. You will be okay exploring for today, won't you?"

The children nodded. "We can play Super-Zappers," said Bean, "we may even find another one so we can both have a game." Boris explained that he would be in the shed if they needed anything. They wished him success and then he was gone.

"He's really nice," observed Peanut, swinging her legs to and fro on her chair. "I wish I had known to bring the curtain material, it would have made his life so much easier and it would be nice to repay his kindness."

"He's not the sort of person you meet very often," agreed Bean. "Grown-ups usually just tell you not to do the things you want to, and to do the things you don't want to. They make up so many rules that you cannot possibly remember them all. Then they wonder why you are being naughty and get all angry with you. Do you realise that Boris didn't lose his temper once yesterday?"

"I know," said Peanut, "let's clear away the breakfast things then go and explore."

As they stood however, the table cleared itself. Peanut had to step out of the way of a plate of toast. Most unusual. "I wondered what Boris meant earlier when he said we all have self-cleaning ovens but not many of us had self-cleaning tables," Bean laughed.

"It feels a bit like Christmas, you never know what is going to happen next. Maybe we are not supposed to work today, Boris did say it is Myday. Shall we play and explore then Bean?"

Bean nodded and they stepped outside into the sunlight. As they walked along the rose-bordered pathway they kept their eyes open for another Zapper.

"Good morning," an elephant greeted them. As though it were the most usual thing of all, the children wished the elephant a 'good morning' in return. After all, if the elephant could speak yesterday, there was no good reason why he should not do so today.

Outside the gate stood two small ponies. One was grey with a beautiful long flowing mane. The other was chestnut. "Would you like a ride?" they asked the children.

"Oh, yes please," they replied.

"We are going over the river today to visit our parents and Boris said you might like to come along. We waited a while just in case you showed up," said the grey, "the grass here looked very edible anyway so we had breakfast while we waited."

The children climbed up and once correctly seated, they set along the path through the forest. "Hold tight," warned the ponies. Peanut, who had never previously ridden, clutched at the mane of the poor grey for dear life. "You can relax just a little Peanut, I will be careful."

Travelling at a gentle trot, Peanut became used to being bumped about and decided she didn't mind so much after all. "Weee," she cried and grinned across at Bean. As if on cue, the ponies gathered some speed, galloping along the mossy pathway, kicking up small clods of earth as they travelled. The breeze streamed through the children's hair and colour visited their cheeks. Bean overtook, the chestnut was the natural leader, having longer legs.

Swiftly they passed other cottages and many trees. Peanut caught sight of a really strange looking beast in one of the gardens. It had four heads, a large snail shell and numerous legs. The reason it stood out though was because it was five different colours. If you put five different animals into a cement mixer and switched it on, the finished article would possibly look similar.

Peanut almost forgot to hold on to the mane. "What was that creature?" she asked.

"A craminal," yelled back Bean's chestnut. "It's an animal which cannot decide what it most wants to be and so chooses to be everything it thinks it might like."

"Freaky," said Peanut.

"Wow, look Peanut," called Bean from ahead. Right in front of them was the riverside and it looked absolutely breathtaking. The children slid to the ground and thanked the ponies who promised to return after their visit home.

Six baby rabbits were playing a game of skittles with fir cones. Their mother looked on. All around her Peanut could see animals and craminals, insects and birds, fish and children. There was so much going on and the entire clearing seemed full of laughter. There didn't seem to be one unhappy creature here. This happiness had been achieved despite the fact that not one television or video game was in sight.

Bean spotted some children playing with Zappers, so he sped over to play while Peanut went for a swim. The water was azure blue and pleasantly warm. "I wish things were like this at home," said Peanut to a similar-aged girl.

"Cheer up," the girl replied, "you can still be as happy or as sad as you decide you want to be, no matter where you are."

"True," Peanut agreed, "but sometimes others can go out of their way to make you unhappy. Then it can be difficult to remain cheery."

"Well that's the time that you just head straight back here, then you find it easier to return and face people like that. Everybody needs somewhere they can just BE." Peanut looked at the girl with interest. Freckles and bright red hair were secondary features to her beaming smile.

They watched Bean with his new friends. Coloured shapes filled the air as their game heated up. He saw them watching and yelled, "I wish Boris was here, we could zap him and he'd have to give us tea!"

The girls left the water and joined in the game. Bean was smothered in paint. The mossy grass was springy beneath their feet as they ran. The game lasted well into the afternoon. When finally they decided they were exhausted they returned to the water for a swim to get clean and refreshed.

After, onto the riverbank they climbed, to lie in the hot afternoon sun until dry. "Why don't you like sport much Bean when you are so obviously good at it?"

"Mum and Dad want me to be an Olympic swimmer or a champion rider. Or I could be a renowned athlete, but what I can't be is marginally interested enough to take part now and again. They are so competitive, even with each other. If one of them wins at something which they enter together, the other goes away to sulk for a week. They cheat too.

I don't want to be like that. It causes so many arguments. Actually, I would like to be something interesting, only I don't know what – yet."

"Have you told your parents?" asked Peanut.

"No," said Bean, "I have never had the chance. They just keep on entering me in different events. When I don't win they get angry. They say I don't try hard enough."

There was a rush of hooves. The ponies had returned to collect them. Standing up Peanut stretched; "Hey, this is supposed to be a rest, let's enjoy it as much as we can." They waved to everybody as they started back along the path to the cottage.

When they arrived back, the children first went to the kitchen to see if Boris was there. "I will check upstairs if you grab us a drink," Peanut ran up the stairs and called along the corridor but there was no reply.

Back in the kitchen, they thirstily drank a glass of water, then went to see if they could locate Boris's shed.

"Ever seen an inside-out daisy?" asked an elephant. The children hadn't but they were in no rush, so they waited while the elephant plucked a daisy from the grass to show them.

"Thank you, have you seen Boris today?" Bean asked, peering at the daisy.

Its stem was poking through the centre of the yellow middle, instead of emanating from the back.

"He could be in there," the elephant said, pointing with his trunk to the end of the garden where a large shed stood, surrounded by odd bits and pieces, "there have been strange noises coming from that direction all day."

"Thanks for showing us the daisy, it's very odd!" said Bean. Then to Peanut, "he must have been in there all day." They walked across and knocked on the door. There was no reply. "Boris, are you in there?" Peanut called.

The children stood and waited. Silence was their only reply.

"Boris?" called Bean. He turned the door handle slowly. "Boris?" It was unlocked, but as the door swung open they saw a very odd sight.

There in front of them, was Boris. He was hanging upside-down from the rafters by his feet. Gently he swung backwards and forwards with a look of complete concentration on his face. His long cloak was gently sweeping small piles of dust to either side of the shed. At the far end of the room was a very scientific-looking experiment. There were glass tubes and boiling liquid. Every thirty seconds or so a metal lid lifted off a glass container and from it emanated a loud *beep*. Then out dropped a small package, wrapped in brown paper and tied with string. There was a whole mound of them already sitting there.

"I don't think he heard us," whispered Bean to Peanut. "Don't you think we should let him know we are here?"

"Em, well..." she began, looking at Boris swaying.

"Boris, we're back," he shouted.

"Em, no I don't really think"... replied Peanut at the same time. Too late! Boris lost concentration so completely that his feet slipped from the beam above and he smashed to the floor. Huge piles of dust flew up into the air and they all began to cough and sneeze, including Boris, who was rolling around the floor, trussed up into a tight ball of cloak. Frantically he tried to find his way out then suddenly a head popped out of the ball.

"Sorry Boris," said Bean with a bashful grin, "I didn't think."

"Oh, don't worry my boy," Boris accepted, trying to stand up, "I had to come down anyway."

Peanut giggled. "What were you doing?"

"I have to get everything ready for my lecture tomorrow," he replied, putting the packages into a large box, "come and help would you? I seem to have lost track of time."

The children knelt beside the box. *Beep* went the machine. Plop went a package as it fell on to the pile.

"What sort of lecture is it that requires you to hang upside down from a beam?" asked Peanut doubtfully.

"Well, It is Yourday tomorrow, as you know. Everyone helps other people by doing something for them that they may like. During the course of the week some children asked exactly how bats hang upside down. They want to know why they do it and whether we could do it if we wanted to. I've been thinking about it ever since."

"How do you do it then Boris?" asked Bean with interest. Peanut looked up.

"That's just it. I know they hang upside down to sleep and that they can stay there comfortably and safely for as long as they wish. What I didn't know was if I could do it safely. Though I found it quite restful up there," he added rubbing a lump that was beginning to show on his head, "I'm still wondering about safety!" He put more packages into the box. "These should help."

"What are they?" asked Bean.

"Undo one if you like," Boris said. He stood up to get another empty box. Peanut continued to pile packages in containers while watching Bean. Inside was what looked like a small black square of rubber.

"What does it do?" Bean asked.

"Sit down lad and rub it on the soles of your shoes." Bean did as he was told. "Mind you put it on thickly," advised Boris, "we don't want any more accidents," he grinned. When Bean had done this, Boris told him to walk around a little, then once he got the hang of it to try and walk up the wall and across the ceiling. Peanut had stopped packing the box and was watching closely.

At first, Bean could hardly move his feet at all. They seemed to be sticking to the floor and it took a mighty effort to pull a foot upward before replacing it to the ground. It really made his legs ache. Slowly, he learned that if he squished his foot to the left then the right as he tried to lift it, his foot came away quite easily.

Next he stared straight ahead at the wall. Squish thud, one foot began climbing. Squish thud, he placed his left foot above the right one. They stuck well to the wall, but Bean realised he would have to climb quicker so he didn't lean backward towards the floor. Squish thud, squish thud, he ran until he met the ceiling. Now completely upside down he carefully moved to the centre, avoiding the light bulb also hanging there, as it should. "Brilliant!" said a triumphant Bean.

Peanut applauded his performance. She turned to Boris, "Can we come with you to your lecture?" she asked.

"Of course you can," Boris replied looking mighty pleased. When Bean managed to climb down again, he helped to finish the packing. Then they took them back to the cottage kitchen, where they stacked them on the floor. To her astonishment, Peanut realised that she was actually hungry. "Must be all that fresh air today Peanut. Time to eat I think." Boris waved his arms in the air and tea fell to the table. "Ha!" he cried, "sometimes I can't do it, but sometimes I can!"

Chapter Five

Once they had cleared away Peanut said she wouldn't mind investigating the bookshelves in her room. With so many as yet unread books there, she just had to make a start. Boris also fancied a spot of reading, leaving Bean who was so tired, he decided it was time to go and get some rest.

Reaching her room, Peanut closed the door and looked at all the books. Which one? She wandered from one end of the bookcase to the other reading the titles from the spines.

On the bottom shelf she realised that all the books had children's names on them. She pulled out one entitled simply 'Poppy'. She flicked through the pages to the end where many of the pages were absolutely blank. Replacing it on the shelf she chose one from further along. This one was called 'Peanut.' The cover was blue and it had a little curly gold line around the border. She was both surprised and pleased to find a book with her name on it.

Settling down onto her bed she began to read. The book was about her and life back home with Oliver and Ida! She stopped reading as a thought entered her mind. Turning to the back of the book she discovered that this book also had blank pages at the end of it.

She took it back to the shelf and chose another, which looked like a storybook. This one was called 'Yo-yo on my ankle' by Arthur Leg. Two hours later there was a knock at her door.

"Come in," she called and in walked Boris with a tray.

"Would you like some hot chocolate Peanut? I just took one to Bean and he is in the middle of a book called 'Trains for beginners."

"Yes please." She took a mug from the tray. He wished her goodnight and went towards the door.

"Boris," she called, "who is Poppy?"

Boris sighed, then turning he went to sit beside Peanut's bed.

"Poppy turned up here one Funday, about four years ago. She was almost exactly like you. Her parents were farmers and they thought nothing of making her do all the work on the farm. She used to wake at 4 a.m. and not get back to bed until midnight. She had to start by milking the cows, then clean out the sheds and sties, and feed animals. Once she was mucking out the bull's shed when she was thrown high into the air by the evil creature's horns. Her leg was broken, but when she managed to get to her parents they told her to stop moaning. They wanted her to get on with the work and told her to stand on one leg and finish the task. Later she managed to get to a doctor and he put her leg in a cast. Her parents were furious when they found out. They said she was an attention seeker and sent her to bed with no supper. That was when she first came here." he sighed, then he continued:

"Poppy loved reading. She taught herself to read from the Farmers' Gazette, because her parents wouldn't let her go to school. I think they needed her at home so they wouldn't have to employ any staff. One Sadday, Poppy returned home because she knew her parents wouldn't be able to cope without her. She was such a nice little girl."

"You speak about her as though she no longer exists." Peanut noted.

"Well, she probably doesn't," Boris sighed again, "she was only nine years old and they were giving her the work of twenty fully grown men. It wouldn't surprise me if she died of overwork, if not of neglect."

"Why don't you get in touch with her?"

"I can't. I cannot go to your world. If Poppy could have returned, surely she would have done by now. She would have been 13 years old now. Something must have happened to her," he stated gloomily. "Anyway, you should be asleep by now," he stood up.

"You can't go there, but I can," Peanut said.

"Peanut, I don't want to find out how she is at you expense. It's not right."

"Look Boris, you have been very kind but you have to know that I won't sit by and let another child suffer. I have to get the curtain remnants for you anyway. I may as well do both these tasks at once. From what you say anything could have happened to Poppy." (As it turned out she was right!). She took a gulp of her not-so-hot chocolate. "The more I think about it, the better the idea seems."

Peanut wriggled a little further down into her covers, there's something about warm chocolate and warm covers that makes you feel secure. "Another thing," she added looking Boris straight in the eyes, "with your help, I may be able to help other children too. You told me I earned three wishes, do they work back in my world?"

"Yes" Boris nodded cautiously, "Peanut, this is serious. You could be hurt or killed. What sort of person would I be to allow this?"

"How would you feel if Bean would come with me. He still has his wishes to use. Together, maybe we could succeed. I have to return at some time anyway. Mummy and Daddy don't know where I am and to be honest, I'm in a bit of a sticky situation back home which I ought to sort out," she confided.

Boris looked at Peanut's honest face. Her eyes were shining and her expression was hopeful. "We would have to plan it properly. Give me time to think this through, Peanut," he asked, "goodnight little one, sleep tight." Taking the tray he left the room quietly closing the door behind him.

Peanut got out of bed and went to the window. The nearby branches were waving gently in the evening breeze, the world seemed somehow at peace. She yawned and returned to bed where quickly she fell into a deep slumber and dreamed of rainbow fruit and tropical beaches.

Chapter Six

The next morning Peanut was the first to reach the kitchen. She made a pot of tea and placed mats onto the table. Next she took down the orange coloured mugs from the dresser and got some cutlery. As she was making the toast Bean walked in. "Hello," she grinned.

"Hello yourself," he yawned, "couldn't you sleep or something?"

"Very well actually," she replied, putting eggs, bacon and tomatoes into the frying pan.

Bean poured the tea and heated some plates. They were just putting breakfast onto the table when Boris came downstairs. He looked very pleased, "Good morning," he said, with eyebrows raised and eyes wide in amazement, "breakfast made, ready and waiting. Coo, this hasn't happened to me since Poppy left."

The children were pink with pride. They all sat down. "Has Peanut told you of her idea yet Bean?" Boris asked.

"Not yet," she said. Then over breakfast and lots of cups of tea they all discussed the matter in some depth. Before anybody could mention Bean accompanying Peanut on the rescue mission, he said he too would like to be there. So that took care of that! Eventually it was decided that they would leave together on Sadday.

Later that day they all went to the Land of Odd lecture hall. It was packed. There were chairs in neat rows, starting at the little podium at the front of the hall, spreading right the way to the very back. Almost every seat was taken. Obviously there was a lot of interest in this subject. Animals, craminals and children chattered to each other as they eagerly awaited Boris's lecture.

Peanut and Bean squeezed onto the end of a crowded row. They had to share a seat between them. Boris walked purposefully to the podium with his cloak billowing out around him.

"Doesn't he look important?" whispered Bean to Peanut. She was squashed up against an old man whose jacket seemed to be full of small animals. They were all speaking at once trying to compete with the sheer volume of the crowd. Peanut looked at Bean blankly, she couldn't hear what he was saying. She frowned and shrugged.

"I said *doesn't he look important?*" Bean repeated in a louder voice.

"Pardon?" questioned Peanut. From the podium, Boris waved his hand for silence.

"Doesn't he look important?" Bean bawled yet again to a completely silent room.

"Thank you," Boris acknowledged from the podium. Bean blushed and inched down in his seat so as not to be seen by all the inquisitive faces turned towards him. The lecture on bats began.

Toward the end, Boris requested that all the chairs be moved back to give him some room. Amid much noise this was achieved. He leaned down and rubbed the soles of his shoes, then confidently strode up the wall and onto the ceiling. From there he continued to speak.

The audience craned their necks to see. His cloak hung downwards over his face and his arms waved dramatically as he explained certain points of these fascinating creatures lives. He did try to tuck some of the cloak into his braces so he could at least see his audience to continue.

"In the boxes at the back of the hall," he cried, "are some brown packages. Take one each and use the contents on your shoes or hooves. Please put the paper in your pockets to take to a bin at the end. Could you also coat the feet of your chairs." He waited for this to be done.

"Would you all sit down and place you feet firmly on the floor so we can continue this experiment." Everybody did as they were asked and soon they were ready. Once Boris could see the entire room patiently waiting, he asked them not to be alarmed.

Freeing his cloak he raised his arms and there was a resounding Boom! The lecture hall turned upside down and an unsecured drum kit standing in the corner, fell to the ceiling.

Boris pointed out that he was up the correct way now and his audiences were upside down. He was just concluding that this could be considered a safe enough occupation if one wished, when his spell let him down.

As everybody came unstuck they began to fall. Screams filled the air, echoing around the hall. Peanut closed her eyes and held her breath, but just as they should have hit the floor something strange happened. Everybody, chairs too, began to float. Bobbing around was truly an odd sensation. People started to laugh with relief and clap. Boris returned the hall to the correct way up.

The wizard looked on in puzzlement. Gradually the chairs landed safely and the passengers all congratulated him on his excellent, stimulating talk. Though flushed with pleasure at all the praise, Boris secretly felt a little embarrassed. He knew his cloak had cast a releasing spell all of its own, but couldn't imagine how everybody had been saved from the dreadful calamity of smashing to the floor.

People began to leave and as the hall cleared, Peanut and Bean went to the front to meet up with Boris.

"What happened?" asked Peanut. "I was really frightened there for a moment, you could have warned us."

"He couldn't," said Bean, "his cloak failed him didn't it Boris?"

"I'm afraid so," he nodded and sighed.

"I used a wish to make people float a while," said Bean. Then glancing at the saddened face of Boris he added, "Cheer up, all's well that ends well."

Peanut and Boris both thanked Bean for his swift thinking and saving the day. Everybody thought it had been planned anyway!

"Is it tea time yet?" asked Bean.

Peanut took the hint and said, "Yes, come on Boris, I'm really hungry now, hurry up." She took his hand and pulled him towards the doorway.

When they reached the cottage, they were all tired. Boris elected that tea be brought by magic to save anybody the job, if the cloak worked. Happily it did. At the end of a magnificent feast Boris said, "Right what shall we do this evening?" He waved his arms and a game compendium fell to the table along with a small green frog. The children were growing used to this behaviour and Peanut stood to open the door and release him.

"Croak, croak. Could you direct me to the nearest croak pond," he said patiently waiting in the doorway.

"Yes you go left at the door, right at the daisy patch, across the lawn, over the rockery and there it is. Large, blue and really cool."

"Thanks dude croak."

"Ludo?" asked Peanut.

"I'm not, it was an accident," said Boris.

"Snakes and ladders," said Bean.

Peanut did not think this a good idea. With a torn cloak it could be an exceptionally dangerous game. So they started on the Ludo. Then Peanut and Bean played Chess. Bean won a watch. It fell to the table at an alarming rate, but luckily he caught it before it landed. Peanut won a clip-on reading lamp for winning a game of Bingo. Then Boris made some hot chocolate for them all, the conventional way.

With the drinks, Boris produced a plate of chocolate chip cookies from up his sleeve. The children thanked him in unison and tucked in to their supper.

"It's Ourday tomorrow, what would you like to do?" asked Boris. "I actually have a family with me this week so maybe we could make the most of it with a picnic? I won't get a chance again for a while as you both leave me soon. Maybe never!"

"Don't be daft, of course you will. In fact you are going to have to build a multi-storey cottage with thousands of bedrooms for when we bring back Poppy... and lots of others."

Bean said, "Or even long dormitories with uniform beds – or should that be beds in uniform? Yes, beds in uniform, tables in casual clothing and walls with ears in sheep's clothing," he laughed.

"I am seriously worried about you two idiots," Boris chuckled. "Shut up, don't you know I am mad enough already without you adding to it. So is it a picnic?"

"Yes please," they chorused.

"Right, wear old clothing so we can climb trees without fear of getting messy."

"We haven't got any," Peanut said as a bag of laundry fell on her head. Red and white striped tights covered her eyes. She parted them so one stripy leg was either side of her face, then she posed. Boris and Bean fell about laughing. A blackbird hopped out of the bag.

"Well I for one, cannot see what is so funny," he chirruped, "I could have been seriously injured in a fall like that." He hopped off the table and left haughtily by the door.

Peanut finished her chocolate, tights still dangling. "Boris, you really must try to be more careful."

"I know, but can I truly trust the judgement of a poor deranged girl who wears tights on her head?"

Peanut immediately pulled the garment off, but they were all in fits of laughter now.

"Like parents, like daughter," observed Bean, "after all, they wear veggies on their heads don't they?"

Eventually, they were so sleepy that it was all they could do to get ready for bed.

Chapter Seven

The morning dawned beautifully bright. When Bean awoke he could hear Boris in the kitchen and Peanut singing in her room. He put his feet over the edge of the bed and lazily felt for his slippers with his toes. Finding them, he tried to get the slippers safely on without actually looking at what he was doing. This was always a good game because it gave you time to wake up properly before having to stand up.

"Come on Bean, don't you want any breakfast?" asked Peanut from the doorway. Bean fell off the bed. He'd been so engrossed in his game that he hadn't heard her arrive.

"You okay?" she asked as he re-appeared from behind the bed.

Bean rubbed his leg. "A bit bruised I think and my leg fell off, but apart from that I'm fine. Please don't trouble yourself," he added in mock agony, "I'll manage." Then he had to duck from the pillow Peanut threw. "Ha," he gasped, "I can't even die in peace around here."

Peanut returned to her room for another pillow. Boris came up to see what all the noise was about. There then ensued the most enormous battle that everybody won except the carpet. This was covered in feathers. Bean's pillow sagged emptily in his hands.

"Champions, lead on to breakfast!" Boris yelled.

Peanut took up an imaginary flute and piped marching music. Bean grabbed his slippers and pushed them firmly on to his feet. Then he followed, beating an imaginary drum. All the way along the passage and down the narrow staircase they played, then, "Champions, be seated," Boris yelled and they all sat down to breakfast. Bacon and eggs vanished in a matter of seconds followed by toast, jam and mugs of tea.

For their picnic they decided to visit the play centre which Boris told them had a large indoor and outdoor area where you could play. Plus picnic tables where you could eat. When he mentioned it had been Poppy's favourite place, they couldn't wait to see it.

On arrival at the play centre good smells of barbecuing food greeted them. Happy voices were all around.

Boris led the way. "Where would you like to start?" he said, leading the way, "how about an aeroplane ride?"

The children nodded, trying to take it all in. There were rides of every shape and description. Happily there wasn't a queue in sight so they were soon being strapped into a three-seated glider. A bell sounded and the plane jerked into life, moving slowly at first, then the extending rod pulled the plane up and up.

"My tummy has gone funny," giggled Peanut.

"Mine too," agreed Boris grinning. "It's good isn't it?"

"Weeee!" exclaimed Bean who was sitting in the front seat.

The gliders went all the way around an enormous field; undulating gently but flying so swiftly it quite took your breath away. From this vantage point they could see all the other rides pass below, which gave the children a good introduction to the play centre's outdoor pursuits.

The sun was dazzling overhead and the breeze whipped through their hair (except Boris, whose head was rather more aerodynamic).

At the end of their ride, a tiny old gentleman released them. He had a blue cap pulled down over his eyes. Boris tapped Peanut on the arm "Your turn to choose little one," he said.

"The slide," she clapped her hands grinning, then headed off towards the huge multi lane ride. They grabbed sack mats at the base of the escalator that took them up to the top. Peanut placed her mat on the red lane. "Race you down," she cried.

Bean grabbed the nearest lane, which happened to be his favourite colour, blue, while Boris took the green. They pushed off and down they raced. Peanut had chosen the swiftest, slippiest lane but Bean was heavier which helped him to make haste. Boris was way behind them, but he didn't mind. It was great fun and they went on a few more times before electing for 'Duck the Hippo.' They got very wet when Bean, who was an excellent aim, managed to release the chair on which the hippo sat.

They all cheered when the hippo fell into the water (including the baby hippo wallowing in the swirling muddy water). Twice more the hippo went in. Once, courtesy of Bean and once by Boris. Peanut didn't manage to hit the catch, but she still laughed when the others did. All day they played, stopping only at mid-day to eat ravenously of their wonderful picnic.

At the end of the day, they took their prize vouchers to a kiosk and traded them in for ice-creams all round and a huge red bear.

"That was amazing Boris," Peanut said on their walk home. She was still eating her mint chocolate cone that was beginning to melt.

"What is tomorrow Boris?" asked Bean popping the last of his double strawberry cone into his mouth.

"Theirday. We go to help somebody with a task."

"Who will we be helping?" asked Peanut. They stopped by a footbridge over a trickling stream.

"Well you see that cottage over by the trees?" Boris indicated with an ice-cream covered index finger. The children nodded. "That is where Mrs Batty lives. She makes the most delicious lemon buns and honey fudge."

"Mmmm," Bean slurped.

"You can't still be hungry idiot," Peanut teased thumping him playfully on the arm.

"Why not?" he grinned mischievously.

"Oh your stomach," she began indignantly.

Boris continued, "She needs some help with her roof. With my cape being what it is right now I don't really want to risk trying magic on it. It could have disastrous results!"

Peanut nodded, "That could be very bad."

"So will you help?"

"What needs to be done?" asked Bean, scrunching up his eyes to try and see the roof in the glare of the afternoon sun.

"Last week a branch broke off the tree next to the dwelling. Unfortunately for Mrs Batty, it fell through her roof. She hasn't been able to use the upstairs rooms all week. She has had to sleep downstairs on the couch. Any rain can presently go straight through into her room, which does quite a lot of damage even in a short space of time. She is also fed up at having to keep making up a bed on the sofa every night, then every morning un-making it. She says that after seventy-five years of doing things the other way around she's too old to be changing now! Can't say I blame her."

"Boris, I have never mended a roof before, will you tell me exactly what needs to be done?" asked Bean. He shifted the large red teddy prize to his other arm.

"I'm a bit worried about being up there, I have never climbed a ladder before, let alone fixing something from the top of one," Peanut said.

"The three of us should manage admirably but if you don't want to climb, you could always pass things up to us," Boris said. "Mrs Batty is such a lovely person. She has the sweetest dog too. He is called Boots."

"Let's do it, we can learn as we go along," Bean suggested.

"Righty-ho, you two go on and get the kettle on, I shall just pop in to see Mrs Batty and let her know we shall be calling early tomorrow."

The cottage kitchen was delightfully cool after the warming walk home. Both children had caught the sun a little. By the time Boris got home, tea was on the table and the teddy was resting in the armchair. All he had to do was wash his hands and sit down. Sliced honey-roast ham and salad sandwiches sat in the centre of the table invitingly; tea was steaming in the mugs.

"What did Mrs Batty say?" asked Bean.

"She's expecting us nice and early. We can have breakfast there. She says it will be a treat to be able to look after some company and a pleasure to get the roof fixed." Boris sat at the table. "So it's straight to bed after a bath tonight, or you will never wake in time!"

"Good," yawned Peanut, "it was an excellent day but I am sleepy already. Bags I have the first bath."

Chapter Eight

The next morning, they left the cottage early and set out towards the river and Mrs Batty's cottage. The grass at the side of the verge was still glittering with dew and Peanut's canvas shoes soon became wet. She didn't mind though. The sunshine was already quite hot and cool feet would help to keep her temperature down.

Boris and Bean walked a little way ahead of her carrying some tools. Mrs Batty apparently had quite a good tool supply of her own. Peanut carried the box of nails and tacks etc. She rattled it in time to her steps and a tune that was running through her mind.

They met a family of horses on their way to helping some craminals fix their stable. Later a litter of saddle-backed piglets went by on their way to the Friesian calves' watering area, to assist in digging it out more. Peanut stopped rattling the tin.

"Does Mrs Batty live alone?" she asked.

"Apart from Boots, who I am told is a very good companion."

"Did she not marry?" she asked, drawing level with Boris.

"Yes, she did. Mr Batty was a funny man, with a wonderful sense of humour. Unfortunately he died a few years back. They never had any children. When Poppy was here," he continued, "she used to pop over and help Mrs Batty whenever she needed it. Poppy said Batty was exactly the right name for the woman."

"I'm really looking forward to meeting her," said Bean, "especially if she is such a good cook!"

"Well now you can, here she is." Boris nodded towards the

smiling Mrs Batty.

"Hello, good day," nodded Mrs Batty. Boots was leaping about at their heels. They all greeted her.

"My dears," said the little lady, "it is so good of you to come and help. I've been baking this morning, so you won't go hungry. Looks like it's going to be a lovely day," she chattered on, "so you won't get wet." She nodded her round face up and down. Wisps of grey hair escaped her bun that was perched precariously on the top of her head.

Boots held out his paw toward Peanut. "How do you do?" she said to his solemn face.

"Pleased to meet you," Boots responded with dignity.

"The ladder is in this shed here," said Mrs Batty, pulling open the creaky door. "Saws and hammers are in the rack up there," she pointed. "The bathroom is at the back of the cottage, just through the kitchen and if you need a rest or refreshments just you stop what you are doing and come along in. Don't be shy now, there's plenty here and I'm happy to do it," she chattered, waddling away. "I'm just here in the kitchen, not far away."

Nobody had got a word in edgeways. They stood outside watching her return to the kitchen.

"Okay, let's get tooled-up. Peanut, could you bring a couple of those saws? Bean and I can manage the ladder between us."

The ladder was set against the whitewashed end wall. Bean went up first and Boris followed, having taken the saws from Peanut. Peanut tentatively climbed a few rungs and looked around her to see how high up she was. It wasn't too bad, but she went back down to collect another couple of saws. The larger one she passed up to Boris retaining the other. Up she climbed again.

Bean got to work on one of the larger branches protruding through the roof. He was leaning precariously toward the edge. Once Peanut had managed to get onto the roof, she soon forgot the height and became engrossed in removing some of the smaller branches. She had to keep changing hands with the saw, as it made her arms ache. Every quarter of an hour or so, Boris glanced around to see how the children were doing, and impart advice where it was needed.

"Good grief Peanut, there is a glow coming off your face that would heat a mansion house. Take it easy little one or we'll have to carry you home on a stretcher."

"I do feel rather hot," Peanut stood to stretch her aching back, "I am nearly through another branch. This is the second one," she said proudly pushing her hair back out of her eyes.

"Two? Brilliant!" said Bean. Beads of sweat stood out from his forehead. "When we first got up here I thought we would take all morning just to clear the mess, without fixing a thing. If you carry on at such a speed we will be done in no time." He was about half way through the main branch. "Once this one is done, the worst is over."

They all worked on, sawing and carefully removing the wood as they went. Throwing it to the ground Peanut narrowly missed Mrs Batty below.

"Coo-ee, iced lemonade anybody?" called Mrs Batty, "it's homemade my dears."

That was close, thought Peanut, I could have flattened her, then she grinned at the thought of a flat Mrs Batty. Jamming her saw in the eaves, she dismounted the ladder and took a long cool drink of the delicious lemonade. Boris and Bean were not far behind her.

They took their glasses back to the kitchen. Out of the glare of the early sunlight the kitchen seemed both dark and cool. Mrs Batty chattered away, interrupting herself every now and again with, "Cake – anybody want more cake?"

Boris and Bean tucked into a hearty breakfast of bacon and eggs while Peanut nibbled toast and pumpkin seeds. Bean followed his meal with lemon buns that he pronounced as 'delicious' before disappearing back up the ladder.

Boris whispered to Peanut, "Another one of these biscuits and either I won't be able to get back on the roof, or when I do, I shall be so heavy I will fall straight through!"

"Oh you are all so good. Been wondering what I should do. Worrying about rain coming in and having to keep making a bed on the sofa. So good. Boots, have a bun or more bacon."

"A touch more bacon would be most welcome," replied Boots in his deep growly voice, wagging his tail.

"Back to work," said Boris. They borrowed some wide brimmed hats then, after thanking Mrs Batty for a lovely breakfast, they went outside.

When they returned to the roof Bean was singing; below she could still hear Mrs Batty talking, probably to Boots. They all felt quite lethargic after their meal and work continued at a slower pace. Eventually all of the branches had been removed, leaving the area ready for mending.

Peanut had been thinking about Poppy. "Boris, do you have Poppy's address?" She shook pieces of bark from her hair and clothes.

"Yes, it is in her book on the shelf in your room," he replied and went down the ladder to get some materials. "Throw your saws down, you won't need them any more." Somehow, he managed the ascent with his arms laden with roofing materials and began stacking them to the side of the ladder. There were soft and hard reeds, thatching straw, wire, wire-cutters and mallets. He returned to the ground for cutting shears and paddles.

Boris climbed to the ridge and began to show the children how to use the paddles to get the thatch to one length. While they worked on that, Boris laid cane batons and began to peg the thatch down. Along the ridge he covered the thatch in wire caging to ensure the birds wouldn't just pull it all off again, then he cut the straw.

Peanut and Bean wove reed in and out of the thatch to keep it in place. Soon enough it was time for lunch. The sun was directly above them now. More lemonade was consumed; made from fresh lemons it quenched the thirst much better than the sort the children got at home.

Mrs Batty and her incessant chatter filled the cool kitchen. Lunch was excellent, though Peanut found herself thinking guiltily of home. She wondered what her parents were doing. Bean also thought of home but only because to him there was scarcely enough to eat there. The things that he was allowed to eat didn't seem to fill him up. Fattening things were banned from the house, as they were 'bad for him.' Here however, he was perfectly content to eat the salad providing cheese or ham accompanied it.

Boris watched the two of them while politely nodding every now and again in answer to Mrs Batty. They both looked so different from when they had arrived. Bean was just a little shorter than before – despite his shrinking wish, he was still a growing boy. Also, rather than stooping over in embarrassment, the boy stood up straight. His hair shone and he seemed to smile a great deal more.

Peanut's face shone. Rosy cheeked and without her spectacles her face took on an altogether gentler look. Boris wondered why some parents didn't seem bothered by their offsprings' troubles.

Mrs Batty nudged his elbow and his chin slipped from his hand. With a jolt his musings ended and his attention drew back to Mrs Batty. She was patiently holding a plate of strawberry and cream scones almost under his nose. "Oh my dear, have I tired you already?" She nodded and winked at him. "Miles away you were. I was just telling the children here how these are your favourites." She pushed the plate even further under his nose while nodding at the children for confirmation.

"Mrs Batty, when one cooks as well as you do, everything becomes a persons favourite." Boris said rescuing the situation.

The children agreed whole-heartedly, while Mrs Batty blushed and told them they were too kind.

"Well Mrs Batty," said Boris, "all this eating and chatting isn't going to achieve a very good result on your roof repair now, is it children?"

Peanut wiped some crumbs from her mouth and smiled at Boris as he slowly raised himself to his feet. "I'm finished now Boris. I feel more full than I can ever remember being. Thank you," she added to the kindly lady.

Bean also stood up and thanked Mrs Batty. "We are almost finished up there, but the real test will be when it rains, then we shall see how well the job is done." He grabbed a couple of biscuits and followed Boris and Peanut out of the door.

They continued to bind large bundles of thatch together and clip them in place with wooden pegs, knocking them in with mallets. By mid-afternoon their task was accomplished. They were aching and tired but extremely proud of their work.

They each drank another glass of lemonade before tidying away the tools, and Peanut said, "We shall see how water tight our work is once it has rained tonight."

The children glanced up at the clear sky then threw Boris a questioning look.

Boris smiled, "I don't need to see clouds in the sky to know when it will rain. It rains every night; it is just more convenient that way. Nobody here has to work at night time, there is no need to earn money."

"No money?" gasped Bean.

"No money," agreed Boris, "thus there is no greed or competitiveness and no jealousy. There is sadness enough if somebody dies or on Sadday when some children leave, without us making more for ourselves at other times."

"I think that is a good idea," said Peanut, "but then you would have to have magic to get food and things, or at least a great deal of co-operation."

"Things cannot go on forever as they are at the moment. But I can't see magic or co-operation happening in our world," Bean mused.

"Well now, what we can't change we must learn to accept," said Boris, "which is why you must enjoy every moment you are here. It will give you the strength to face things back home."

Mrs Batty was elated that the roof was mended. She asked them all to stay to tea. They were thanked repeatedly but the real reward was in the feeling of achievement. They talked and laughed all through tea until it was time to go 'home'.

Mrs Batty and Boots stood at the door. "It was so lovely to have company, you are always welcome, come again if you have time." Bean complimented her cooking again and Mrs Batty positively glowed with pleasure. Half way down the path, Peanut returned to quickly tell Mrs Batty that she was going to find Poppy and not to worry any more.

Mrs Batty looked concerned. Peanut took the old lady's wrinkled hand "I know you miss her," she added in barely more than a whisper "You know I have to try to find her." Mrs Batty nodded in understanding, and then she kissed her cheek and wished her luck. "Poppy is special to me and I wish you a safe passage." Then she waved as Peanut ran back to join Bean and Boris.

If we had no money at home, my Dad wouldn't have a job; nobody would need a bank, thought Peanut. She wondered if he would be any better tempered. Then she thought of Poppy's parents and wondered if they would be less uptight and angry too.

"You're quiet, Peanut," said Bean.

"Yes," said Boris. "Come along little one, worrying never helped anybody. What can we do to cheer you up fair lady?" he asked, gallantly producing a bunch of flowers from his cloak. "For you," he added, bowing low in front of her.

Peanut chuckled and took the flowers. "Why thank you, kind

Sir," she mimicked his old worldly charm.

"I spy with my little eye," started Boris.

"Unfair," called Bean from ahead, "we could never win that one, we don't know all the names of everything yet."

"True," agreed Boris, "well, let's at least keep you looking forward. What about tomorrow?"

"What's tomorrow?" chorused the children together.

"Friendsday," replied Boris, "goodness I think I ate too much tea."

"You ate too much at breakfast and lunch too," laughed Peanut.

"Well, if I ate too much, what about Bean?"

"I'm too full to want to think about that," grinned Bean patting his tummy.

Boris took out his handkerchief and wiped a dirty smear from Peanut's forehead. "There you go tatty head."

Bean bent down and picked a blue and green striped flower. "Look Peanut, what's this one Boris?"

Boris turned. "Oh, that is just a Perrigreen. There are lots of them here, especially near meadows. If you look over there," he indicated a nearby field with a nod of his head, "you will see all sorts of flowers, wild flowers and weeds."

The children looked at the field and indeed there was a profusion of colour and life.

The children eventually decided that they would like to wait at home and see who visited them. Boris explained that in order to receive visitors they must raise the yellow flag to the top of the mast so everybody could see they were at home. Had they chosen to go visiting others instead, they would need to raise the red flag. There could be nothing worse that going to visit people only to find them not home.

That decided, they went to take a closer look at the field before going home. Peanut made some small posies of flowers ready for the next day while Bean had his first ever encounter with a baby craminal, closely watched by the craminal's mother. Once they had skirted the meadow Boris pointed out his cottage. They hadn't realised this was the back way home.

They passed a fox with her family and bid them a good evening, then went around to the front entrance, past the upside-down tree. Arriving just as the sun was setting, they turned to watch the colourful glowing pinks, mauves and orange. Peanut went to put the posies in water while Boris put the kettle on for cocoa.

Bean started to tidy up a little, ready for the next day. He peered into the corner of the 'L' shaped kitchen.

"Would you like some light Bean?"

"I looked for a light switch and when I couldn't find one assumed there wasn't any," Bean explained.

"There isn't a light switch, you just have to request a light if you need one." Boris returned to his cocoa making. "Light, please," he said in an ordinary voice. The kitchen took on a wonderful warm glow. The children looked around in amazement. Everything was beautifully lit up.

"Glow worms," announced Boris proudly, "these are a bit larger than the ones you get back home but pollutant free! We do have a generator that converts the wind and rain power, but the glow-worms make things so picturesque. Your cocoa is ready when you are." He grabbed a biscuit barrel. "Help yourself."

"Not likely," said Bean, "I know when I'm beaten." They took their cocoa to bed. Peanut tried very hard to stay awake long enough to see it rain. But when the first drops fell against the window, she was already fast asleep.

Bean was also tucked up and fast asleep. The only person awake was Boris. He tried to work out a safe rescue plan, but sleep finally got the better of him.

Chapter Nine

Boris was the first to the kitchen the next morning and after a couple of mishaps he managed to magic a breakfast of boiled eggs, soldiers and a stack of toast. While setting the table he put out some dishes of Mrs Batty's homemade jams and sunny. Finally he added a pot of hot tea but the children still hadn't emerged.

Boris opened the kitchen door and shouted up the stairs. He heard a thud followed by footsteps, and then Peanut appeared bleary eyed at the top of the stairs. "Sorry Boris," she said, "I didn't realise it was morning already. I'll be right down."

"Okay little one, would you give Bean a knock too?" Boris returned and sat in the kitchen.

"I can see all that fresh air and good food yesterday gave you a wonderful sleep," Boris commented once the children appeared.

"I certainly slept well," agreed Peanut. Bean just yawned and nodded as he tucked into his breakfast.

There were a few things to be tidied and a flag to raise before visitors could arrive, so Boris began to clear away some of the breakfast things as they were used.

"Is there no school here?" asked Bean between mouthfuls.

"Now let me see, what would we need school for?" We can all cook and sew. We can all grow vegetables and flowers. Our parents impart all sorts of life skills but family or friends can teach arithmetic. For science we have an amazing laboratory where anybody can go and try out a few experiments – just as you have libraries where you can read books." Boris explained.

"Adults teach children to read and children remind adults to laugh and see things with fresh eyes."

Peanut spread some lamalade on toast. She frowned, "I can use a computer but I had never thatched a roof before yesterday," she acknowledged.

"Precisely! Can either of you cook?" Boris asked.

"Not much, breakfasts or snack food."

"I have seen you do breakfasts, but that is more than a lot of children can manage. Crafts and trades are started young. Theoretically, I could build a cottage when I was your age. Though of course I wouldn't even have been able to lift some of the materials, so it wasn't likely to physically happen!"

"What about things like history and geography?" enquired Bean.

"History is passed on in the form of bedtime stories. Geography is done by travelling around and finding out in groups or pairs. We have a great deal of fun, but there are lots of books to help you along. Everybody older than nineteen is a teacher of something. Some are younger. We all have knowledge and love to share."

"No television you see? We are all too busy living our lives to the full without needing to watch others live theirs. Had you previously heard of the Land of Odd?"

"I have a map of the world," Peanut noted, "but no, I cannot remember seeing the Land of Odd on that map."

"That was a trick question actually," Boris said mischievously. "We haven't been discovered yet, except by certain children of course" he added.

Boris sat down again. "We know all about your world. All of us can visit you while we are under the age of twenty, just to experience your lifestyle a little. None of us have so far chosen to remain there. There is just too much noise and aggravation. We swiftly grow homesick."

"The craminals can't visit, they are too obvious. One was caught and told he was to be put in a laboratory so he could be experimented on. Luckily he was able to wish himself home. I would have loved to see their faces once they realised he had escaped a secure unit. I fully expect your government have a secret file on it."

"I saw a documentary on television once about UFO's," said Peanut, "according to them it is not in the public's interest to know."

They finished breakfast. Boris waved his cloak to clear the last few things away and clean the kitchen in readiness. A toast rack and the teapot obliged, washing and putting themselves away. The rest however just floated gently around the kitchen, much to the children's amusement.

"The sooner we get that cloak mended the better," Peanut giggled at the bewildered look on Boris's face. Both children helped and soon got the kitchen clean. Unfortunately Boris tore his cloak further on the cupboard door when he went to get the flag out. He explained that the cloak became weaker each time it was damaged but insisted he could still manage.

They unrolled the yellow flag and both children took a corner while Boris fastened it to the hoist. Then they helped hoist the flag until it fluttered merrily in the breeze. Once it was secure the three returned to the kitchen. They hadn't been there very long when a babble of voices could be heard from the pathway.

"Hello, it's Mrs Batty!"

"Herrumph," said Boots.

"Sorry Boots, it's Mrs Batty and Boots," amended Bean, "how is the roof?"

"Yes my dears, quite wonderful. I had the most wonderful sleep. We thought we should call and let you know. We met up with Pa Baddle and his family at your gate."

"Come along in all of you," Boris invited.

"Heard you had children here, so we have come along for a natter," Mr Baddle explained.

Pa Baddle beamed at the children. He was a thin man with thick black curly hair, a long black pointy beard, black rimmed spectacles and bright shiny eyes. Peanut just knew he was fun by the look of him.

Ma Baddle, by complete contrast, was round with straight blonde hair sticking out at all angles. There were three children. Mary who obviously took after her father (minus the beard), Toby who looked like both parents with straight black hair and little baby Jev Baddle who had blonde curly hair and bright blue eyes.

Noise and games ensued in a never-ending, ever-changing social whirl. New people arrived. Some moved on to their next visit. The teapot was emptied many times and the kettle seemed to be forever boiling. Food of all descriptions was procured, magicked or brought. Peanut's face ached from smiling and her belly ached from laughing. Her mind ached from all the new faces and names.

Bean forgot to be self-conscious and just enjoyed, then enjoyed some more. As the last visitor left the cottage a red backed buckle-bum (very rare in the Land of Odd), walked by and greeted the children. He handed them two amazing red eggs and told them to be very careful with them, but he wished them to enjoy their gift. With that he was on his way again.

Boris put the red eggs into an incubator. "You will have to wait a year before these are ready to hatch, so it is better if we put them in straight away. You are honoured to have been chosen, I can tell you." It was a perfect end to the most amazing day.

They went to lower and collect the flag, rolling it safely for the next Friendsday. "That was a brilliant day Boris," Peanut said.

They went into the garden for a little walk around. Boris said, "I almost hate to bring the subject up, but we need a rescue plan for tomorrow. Since you have your minds set on rescuing Poppy, I drew these up to help." He handed them maps, pulled from his pocket and indicated a large red X. "This is the farm where Poppy lives. I should start there," he said. "I have done my best to remember smaller details such as the position of the bull shed and the nearest friendly face from Poppy's point of view. He pushed his fingers through the middles of his head where his hair used to be. "One each, just in case you become separated, but my advice is to stick together. Promise you will try to minimise risks, I want to see you both again… safe."

"Boris, we can't minimise the risks. The whole idea is a risk," said Bean.

Boris proceeded, "There are other details from the book upstairs that I thought might be helpful. I have jotted down as many of these as would fit on the back of the maps." He waved his cloak and a grandfather clock and a torch fell out. "Discard the clock, it was supposed to be a watch. I couldn't actually think of a plan," he said.

"Now, if you move slightly back from the debris. I am determined to get this right." He concentrated hard. One pedal car, a shoehorn, three speedometers and one standard lamp later Boris triumphantly handed each of them a compass, a watch and a torch.

That night the children took their cocoa up to bed with them early so they could get a good night's sleep before their departure. Boris told them he wouldn't be there to say goodbye in the morning as he would be busy, so he wished them both well and told them he would await their speedy return.

Peanut hugged the Wizard and went into her room. Bean thought about shaking Boris by the hand, but hugged him too, because it felt more fitting to do so.

Chapter Ten

Sadday dawned as bright as any other morning, but it was with a heavy heart the children forced down breakfast. Peanut took one last look around the kitchen. "Shall we go to my house first to get the remnants, Bean, what do you think?"

Bean nodded, "We have to start somewhere. Are you ready?"

They put on their watches, then picked up the torches, maps and compasses. They also picked up the chocolate bars that Boris had left for them. Finally they stepped out of the cottage into the beautiful morning. The latch made a very final sounding 'click' behind them.

Along the pathway they looked back, then continued to the upside-down tree where, for them, it had all begun. In one week the difference in each child was amazing. Confident, relaxed and healthy. Boris watched them leave from the upstairs window. He wiped a tear from his face and felt completely deflated. He watched long after they had left. The silence surrounded the old man.

"How do we leave the Land of Odd, Bean?"

"Good question, but I don't actually know the answer. We had better go and find Boris to ask him. Have you noticed just how quiet it is today, I can't even hear bird song."

"Yes," agreed Peanut, "except for the high-pitched whirring sound which is starting to get on my nerves."

Bean put his head on one side. "I can't hear anything," he said. Then, as the sound grew louder it was accompanied by a rumbling noise. The ground seemed to shake beneath their feet. Bean grabbed hold of Peanut's sleeve and not a moment too soon. The ground beneath their feet suddenly opened up and they were falling. Leaves and soil, twigs and other debris fell with them. Bean clung tightly to the sleeve with his eyes firmly shut.

Screaming inside their heads, they kept their mouths firmly closed against the falling soil.

As suddenly as it had all began, it stopped. Peanut stayed very still. She couldn't believe they had not been killed in the landing, but there hadn't even been a bump. Bean opened his eyes and let go of Peanut's sleeve. He brushed the soil from his hair and face in batting movements. "It's raining," he observed.

Peanut opened her eyes. They were sitting in a puddle on a pile of folded marquee. The day was indeed cold, grey and drizzly. They appeared to be in a park or large garden. "Grief!" she said, "I had almost forgotten about this. Ugh!" she said and shivered.

"Come along, we ought to get moving, it will help us to get warm." They stood up and started to walk. "Any idea of where we are?" Bean asked.

Peanut wrapped her arms around herself in order to try and get warm. "Not yet," she replied, "I can see a gate over there, maybe we ought to head for that."

There were very few people around, but as they approached the gate a middle-aged, middle-sized, raincoated man entered the gate closely followed by a white highland terrier who cocked its leg at the gatepost. The man gave the dog lead a sharp tug as he saw the children, as though the dog had never previously attempted that move. He then ignored them.

"Excuse me," said Bean politely. The man still ignored them. "Excuse me," tried Bean again, "could you please tell us where we are?"

The man looked Bean up and down disparagingly and then growled succinctly, "On Mars, I expect." He moved off muttering rude things about kids, bad manners and drugs.

Bean looked at Peanut. "The rain isn't the only thing we forgot about is it?" he asked miserably. "Surely he could see we are not on drugs," he said and his shoulders took on a familiar stoop.

Peanut put a hand on his arm. "Cheer up," she said. "It is probably just the weather. It gets into your very bones and makes you mean. I had forgotten about the smell here. Carbon monoxide, it's car and aeroplane emissions. It must all have an effect on people and their behaviour. He might have just been scared of us or something," she said, searching for a reason that Bean would believe. Then, "Ah look, we are in Norwich, good! My home isn't very far from here."

Out on the streets the pavements were full of brolly-wielding shoppers and college students, despite the rain and the cold. It vaguely occurred to Peanut that she might actually bump into her father. The next thought immediately cancelled the last one. Knowing Oliver he would send somebody else rather than go anywhere in this weather. Exercise just wasn't his thing.

Bean once again grabbed hold of Peanut's arm. She had almost stepped out in front of the traffic. "Idiot, you have to look where you are going now," he exclaimed.

Peanut blinked. "Sorry Bean, I will concentrate." She wondered why her parents liked living in the city with all the noise. The smell and the crowding were enough to drive her straight back to the cottage, but for the task ahead.

They walked right through the city centre, dodging baby buggies and people with spiky umbrellas. They passed the station and eventually walked into Thorpe Road. "Here we are," said Peanut. She led the way up some steps to a front door.

As she put her hand on the large brass handle she turned to Bean. "My folks are big people," she said quietly, not really knowing how to explain everything in one go. She just felt incredibly nervous. Sort of sick in her stomach, remembering that she had gone against her parent's wishes in such a huge way. She turned the handle and pushed the door open. It was wrenched from her hands with almighty speed.

Peanut literally leapt backward, knocking Bean down the steps. He landed on the pavement with a jolt at the same time as Peanut sat with a thud on the step. "Ouch," she cried. There, filling the doorway was the large and very imposing body of Ida Fatness. Hands on her hips and face screwed up in total disgust. She was not impressed. In fact, she could hardly believe that Peanut would dare to openly be so defiant.

Torn between shock and rage at the appearance of this child, sent previously to her room, but now sitting before her, looking for all the world as though she was returning from holiday…

Ida leaned toward Peanut; her chins wobbled as her furious mouth tried to form words. Her eyes bulged and her face was almost purple, but no words came out. Peanut appeared all tanned and glowing. Her face had filled out slightly and the child was definitely taller.

"Where are your glasses?" she finally demanded.

"Why aren't you in your room? How dare you…"

A tirade of words and wrath rained down upon Peanut's bowed head. She sat very still and stared at Ida's boat-like fluffy pink slippers.

Bean had sort of rolled over. Slowly he removed himself to behind the relative safety of next-door's wall. He peered over the top as a large wrestler-style arm shot out of the doorway and literally lifted Peanut into the air.

"I'll teach you to do as you are told," he heard, then the door slammed shut, with Peanut inside.

So, thought Bean, this is the easiest part is it? He put his head in his hands to think. He wasn't quite sure what to do next.

Chapter Eleven

Inside the hallway Peanut was feeling quite scared. Her mother was working herself into a frenzy. "How dare you defy me, girl?" demanded Ida while stabbing a large round index finger into Peanut's ribcage. There didn't seem to be a chance to answer before the next question, then the next.

"Did we bring you up to be so ungrateful, well did we? Who do you think you are? So you think you are big enough now to do just as you like, do you madam? Well, I've got news for you." Ida went on and on, each word punctuated with a sharp prod. Peanut edged backwards, fearfully clinging to the stair rail to stop her from falling over the stairs.

Ida positively foamed at the mouth. "I'm phoning your father."

Poor Peanut! She broke out in a sweat as she stood miserably on the stairs, head bowed and frantically trying to formulate answers to all the questions.

"Stay where you are," Ida ordered. She turned to the kitchen and picked up the telephone, fiercely punching the numbers with a force so great Peanut was amazed the telephone didn't disintegrate.

Peanut stayed where she was, not moving an inch. She hadn't meant to defy her parents, it had just sort of happened. Oh! they would really believe that? – NOT! Grief, this looked really bad.

They hadn't brought her up to be ungrateful, indeed she hadn't even considered her gratefulness. Despite her parents inability to relate to her, Peanut was still certain that deep down, really deep down, they did love her. In turn, Peanut loved them too. She was fed and clothed okay, so from her point of view she was looked after, but still almighty glad that she didn't have to be an adult yet. It looked to be very difficult and in fact quite a numbing experience.

Next, Peanut considered who she thought she was while her mother continued to shout into the telephone, presumably to Oliver. I think I'm Peanut, thought Peanut. I think I am a small girl with big trouble right now. This thought jolted her. Oh dear, what about Bean?

She moved from foot to foot trying to see out of the window to see if he was still there. Then she remembered the curtain material. She glanced up as Ida slammed the phone down and turned towards her. One look at Ida's face was enough to make her look straight back down at the boat slippers. Much safer, she though. Wrong!

"Your father can't come right now but you can bet your bottom dollar that he is furious with you," she imparted. Peanut thought that it would be an odd place to keep a dollar.

"So," Ida continued, "you can get to your room and this time you will stay there." She swung her arm back and cuffed Peanut on the side of

her head, knocking the poor child sideways. Peanut pulled herself up, sobbing and ran up the stairs before she got another one. The thump hadn't hurt that much but the shock and unfairness of it did!

In her room, Peanut closed the door and leant against it. She stayed there a moment for the security of feeling a barrier between her and her mother. She put her hand to her head. It felt very hot where the hand had made contact. It is probably very red she thought crossing the room to her bed. She knelt down and pulled a box out.

Lifting the lid, she took out a piggy bank and her tiny mirror. Yes, her temple was red right into the hairline, and probably under my hair too, she thought. Then, replacing the mirror she pulled the rubber disc from the piggy bank's tummy and emptied quite a lot of coins onto the carpet. Still rubbing her sore head she leaned forward again and felt for another box. Hope there aren't any big spiders under here, she thought. Finally her fingers met with the remnant box.

She tipped the box upside down and the material landed in a pile before her. Picking up a large piece of material she placed the coins in the middle and tied the edges in a knot, making a bundle of the coins. She placed this and the remnants into a carrier bag. Next she found some string and tied it around the bag handles. Opening her window, she looked out. Bean was gone! She leaned out a little further frowning. She couldn't wait much longer, her father would be finishing work soon.

She decided to lower the bag out anyway. Afterwards she closed the window again, then crossed to the door and opened it a little. She could hear Ida in the kitchen. Dare I risk this? But then again, can I afford to wait for Daddy to get home?

She opened the door a little further and slid out onto the landing. Stealthily she lowered one leg onto the top stair. Her knee juddered and she shook. Her heart beat loudly in her head. Fingers gripping the banister, she lowered her other leg. She could see the kitchen door was open. The grandfather clock ticked, her heart banged and a food processor whirred in the kitchen. Ida was singing along to the radio, out of key and without the rhythm of the music being played.

Peanut missed the fourth step because it creaked. Clang! The grandfather clock chimed the hour and Peanut almost leapt out of her skin. Down the stairs she fell, one hand wildly grabbing for the banister. Then, the door opened and in walked a tired and hungry Oliver.

Peanut landed in a crumpled heap at his feet and looked up at him in horror. To make matters even more interesting Ida appeared in the kitchen doorway.

"Really Peanut, I can't be bothered with this sort of annoyance. Can't you keep yourself occupied for one measly week?" Oliver asked impatiently. "I am far too important to be bothering with this sort of thing," he waved his hand vaguely while patting his suit clad tummy, then launched into his speech about just how important he was.

Peanut stayed very still, watching and waiting. Oliver wasn't even looking at her; his eyes were fixed on an imaginary crowd about two feet above her head. With every word his chins wobbled like jelly.

Peanut looked across at her mother to see if she was within smacking distance. No, momentarily safe. She swallowed – grief, how do I get out of this one? Where is Bean when I need him? Just then she noticed that, clutched in Daddy's fat hand along with his briefcase, was her remnant bag.

As Oliver spoke, he changed the bags from hand to hand. "So you see in my line of work I must be seen to be doing only important things and mixing with only important people and you are not at all important are you?" He glanced down at where Peanut lay on the floor and turned his nose up. "Wait a minute, aren't you supposed to be in your room?"

His frown deepened.

"Yes Oliver, that is what I have been telling you dear," chirped her mother from the doorway. "She was to stay there but I found her on our front door step this afternoon," she smiled triumphantly as though tale telling earned her an enormous award. Ida shot Peanut a smug look.

"Well why didn't you keep her there you stupid bat?" Oliver demanded. The smug look vanished. "You deal with it woman, you're her mother, what do you do all day anyway? While we are on the subject, don't throw your litter on the pavement, haven't you any decorum?" Oliver threw the remnant bag at Ida and stomped off to the study where he slammed the door.

Ida spun around at Peanut with fury. "This isn't my rubbish," she shouted at the closed door. Grabbing Peanut's arm, she hauled her to her feet and smacked the poor girl's legs with a resounding 'thwack'.

Tears pricked Peanut's eyes making the room blurry. "Right my girl, it's time you earned your keep. Get our dinner and hurry up; we are tired and hungry. This time, I wouldn't disobey if I were you," she said narrowing her eyes. "Clear up this rubbish," she threw the bag at Peanut and disappeared into the sitting room.

As soon as the door closed Peanut ran to the front door. She pushed her precious bag into a potted shrub on the doorstep for safekeeping. Looking up and down the road there was no sign of Bean. She darted back to the kitchen and looked around for inspiration.

Bean was clever at many things, but rescue missions were not his forte. It takes skill and co-ordination to be athletic, or brain co-ordination to be academically clever. If you don't particularly have either, then you just have to keep trying methodically, which is called 'being practical'.

'Practical' described Peanut very well. Bean however was more athletic which is why he had just scaled a drainpipe. Clinging on tightly with one hand he inched the sash window open. It took an almighty effort, but eventually the window was open wide enough to gain access.

He looked into the room. There was a pink brocade bed spread with frilly edges, a dressing table and mirror with frilly edges and a large frilly-edged wardrobe at one end of the room. He swung himself over the ledge and landed with a muffled thud on the cream wade-through carpet. Tiptoeing across the room he passed a wedding photo of a slim blonde lady smiling up at a slim tall dark man. He opened the bedroom door and listened. When Bean had seen Oliver enter the house, he knew Peanut was in trouble, now he would find her and make sure she was safe.

He had just begun his tiptoeing journey across the landing when a terrible thought hit him. The photo! He went back to the room, forgetting to be quiet and picked it up.

Peanut had said her folks were big people. The only big thing about these people was their smiles and his flaming mistake. "Oh pants!" he cried turning the photo over. There on the back were the names Mr and Mrs Woodstock. "Double pants!" he exclaimed, "I'm in the wrong flaming house." He almost leapt out of his skin when he heard footsteps on the landing.

Terrified, he looked around the room for inspiration. Just in time he jumped inside the frilly mass of perfumed clothes in the wardrobe. Mrs Woodstock walked in and looked around. "Obviously hearing things again," she told herself. But since she was here she may as well take a little nap. She kicked her shoes off and curled up on top of the bedspread facing the wardrobe.

Peanut was about to dish up dinner. She heard her father yelling at her to hurry up. Taking up a cloth she wrapped it around the handle of a boiling saucepan. It was much too big for Peanut to have attempted to carry it but she was intent on straining off the water from the vegetables. Lifting the pan to the sink she began to pour, but the pan slipped from her grasp and boiling water streamed towards her tiny hands…

Chapter Twelve

She was standing at the train station with the carrier bag. She blinked then fainted clean away. Bean caught her up easily and took her across to a bench outside the ticket office. The busy world continued on around the pair until finally Peanut shivered and opened her eyes.

"Are you okay," asked Bean with a worried frown.

"I think so," Peanut nodded. Then, "Yes, I'm fine. I thought I was about to be burned but apparently not."

Bean nodded. "I was in this lady's wardrobe. I thought it was your bedroom I had climbed into, but it was Mrs Woodstock's." She came to have a sleep and I was all cramped up. I didn't know what to do so eventually I used a wish and here we both are," he explained.

"My parents are still waiting for their dinner. I was just dishing up when my hands slipped. They have got a long wait," she giggled. "I have put them on the 'wait-a-diet.' And you were in the wardrobe next door? Some help you are!" she laughed until her sides hurt. Bean joined in; he could see the funny side of it, now they were safe.

"Okay, Bean," Peanut said, "what next? To be honest, I am not as sad to leave as I thought I would be." She hugged her arms around herself to try and stave off the cold.

"I'm starving. We haven't eaten since breakfast and I can smell chips."

"I brought some money with me. We need to be careful with it but I think we can afford chips and train fares." She pulled out her map and looked at it. Bean did the same. "Poppy is here, in Yorkshire," she said, pointing at the map. "We ought to hurry if we are to get the train before dark."

Bean looked around them. "Could we use a wish to get more copies of *'Zap'* in the libraries?"

"It's not that simple Bean. We need to stop children from turning into spies and exploiting the Land of Odd. What we need is a way to get the children who really need help to Odd. If everybody could go to Odd, there wouldn't be anybody left here. I mean who would choose to live here?"

"Maybe if Odd could reach out and take the deserving cases?" Bean asked.

Peanut put a finger to where her glasses used to be. It seemed to aid concentration. "If Odd could reach out through the book to take those who really need their brand of life, then all we have to do is increase the amount of books in publication."

Bean nodded, and sniffed the air. His tummy rumbled.

"Okay, here goes; I wish that *'Zap the Wizard and the Land of Odd'* can be in every book store, library, dentist waiting-room, hospital and school. Also, that Odd can reach out through the book to children in its vicinity who would benefit from being there, even just for a little while." She shivered again and stood up, "How do we know if the wish worked?"

"Let's go to a bookshop and see if they have it," Bean said. They went there first, knowing that they would not be allowed to take food into such a shop. When they opened the shop door, a blast of warm air encompassed them. There was an aged man balanced at the top of a step ladder. He wore a maroon bow tie.

"Do you have *'Zap the Wizard and the Land of Odd'* please?" enquired Bean. The children watched as the man slowly dismounted the ladder and walked across to the fiction section. There he took out a book and held it up. "Yes, here it is," he wheezed.

"Thank you," chorused the children and left the shop and one very annoyed and bewildered man, who had to return the book to its shelf and re-climb the ladder.

"Good," Peanut said, "now we really shall have to stick together. I have two wishes left, but you only have one, Bean."

Inside the fish and chip shop, condensation ran down the huge front window. They queued up and looked at all the different food types in the glass-fronted cabinet. Peanut noticed a sign on the wall, which read 'Fresh fish prices fluctuate daily'. She nudged Bean, "What does fluctuate mean?"

"Search me," he replied, "should we change their sign? It could say 'Fresh fish fluctuates fortnightly forever.' That, of course is the polite version," he added, smirking.

"No, Mr and Mrs Key are really nice, leave their sign alone! Their fish and chips are the best in the whole world," she added knowledgeably. They ordered their chips.

"Hello Peanut," called Mr Key from behind the fryer. "Have those on the house for helping me clean my windows Sunday before last."

"I didn't help," replied Peanut, "I

was just standing there talking to you."

"Excellent talk it was too! Chips are still on the house!" he insisted.

Taking their chips they thanked Mr and Mrs Key. Soon enough they were back out on the pavement, heading for the station through the grey drizzly late afternoon. Bean wondered if they had ordered fish, would that have been free too? Out on the pavement they were pushed and shoved as though invisible. Everybody wanted to get out of the rain, but the complete lack of humanity these people had toward each other was incredible, but particularly toward children.

At the ticket office they purchased their tickets. It was fortunate that they hadn't needed to pay for the chips as they only had just enough money to cover two one-way tickets. They found the correct platform and sat on a bench to eat and wait for their train. The chips were delicious and helped to keep some warmth in the children.

Soon enough they were on the train and feeling sleepy.

"We must stay awake, Bean, we have to change trains soon," Peanut yawned. She took out her map again to check the place where they hoped to find Poppy. 'Snarlham Farm' sounded a harsh name, not the sort of place you would choose to visit on a day trip, for instance.

Bean looked to see if there were any landmarks nearby. Nothing! "Looks as though there are just hills and more hills around the farm. Can you see a train station around Snarlham?"

Peanut looked. "No," she said, "it looks as though the closest one is about nine miles away. Can you believe it?"

They heard the end of the line being announced over the speakers and stood to leave the train. Peanut picked up her bag and left. "Don't you want to visit your parents while we are here, Bean?"

"No, they wouldn't be home yet anyway. They went to the Olympics overseas."

On the platform there was a writhing mass of shoving bodies. It made it really difficult to see where they were supposed to be heading and as a result they almost missed their connecting train.

"This one has a buffet," Bean grinned.

"Oh that's just great! Now we can smell food which we cannot afford, all the way to Yorkshire." As it happened they didn't. Both of them fell asleep within minutes of sitting down. They stayed asleep as the train hurtled through the evening and into the night. Every now and again the train stopped and people got on or off. Most of them didn't even notice the children.

Two and a half hours later Bean awoke with a jolt. Somebody had knocked his arm. He sat up and noticed a boy of about the same age trying to steal the remnant bag.

"Oi! No you don't. You wouldn't want it anyway, it's only bits of material," he exclaimed angrily.

The lad jumped back, "I didn't want noffink anyway, just 'avin a look." He tutted and walked away. Peanut awoke, the bag handle was still over her wrist, but she heard the boys talking and pulled the bag closer.

"Bean, I think we must be almost there. I have just seen a sign saying Coldcrag, so Great Snarlham must be next. It is almost eleven p.m., so we shall need to find somewhere to sleep. Hopefully there will be a barn or something en-route where we can stay warm and dry."

They took a last look at the maps, putting them safely away as the train pulled into the station. The only light was the level-crossing lamp. The wind howled around the tiny station. "What's great about this place? That is what I want to know," shivered Bean staring at the sign.

There was just the one road. One way led back to Coldcrag, the other to Snarlham. "At least we can't get lost out here," Peanut wrapped her arms around her coat. They put their heads down and began climbing the first road incline. Four hills later it began to rain. Sheets of water slashed their frozen faces. They took it in turns to walk in front, keeping the person behind slightly wind and rain free for a little, then swapping over when the leader could take no more. Up and down, up and down. The hills went on seemingly forever.

The barn idea was useless out here. There were no houses and no barns. Eventually Peanut stopped. "Bean," she shouted above the wind, "I can't go on like this. I can't catch my breath," she gasped. Bean turned to protect her, and told her to go backwards for a while. This helped a little but Peanut was tired and freezing. All she wanted to do was sleep. Rescuing somebody wasn't nearly as good as it seemed in books.

Again she stopped. Soaked through to the skin, both children looked terrible. Bean didn't know what to do. He couldn't leave her here and he knew they mustn't stay. "Peanut, you have got to keep going. It can't be that much further. Come on," he insisted.

The next large gust of wind blew Peanut over. She just lay there on the rain-drenched road, not attempting to get up. Bean leaned down and hauled her to her feet. She was unconscious. With an almighty effort, he heaved Peanut over one shoulder, staggering sideways with the weight, then, with gritted teeth, he continued. One foot in front of the other. That is all he thought of, putting one foot in front of the other.

Finally he spotted a mass of shadowy buildings. This is near enough, he thought, relieved. He could hear a dog barking but the lights stayed off. Bean assumed there was nobody home. Leaving the road, he crossed to a large barn and tugged at the door. Inside was heaven. He could smell hay; it must be a hay barn. He closed the door and carried Peanut to the furthest place from the door and put her down.

Sitting beside her he once again pulled out his map to read the back. Apparently, providing they were on the correct road, the first property they would come to was the one where Poppy lived, 'Snarlham Farm.' This must be it then, he shivered. Where was everybody? Glancing at Peanut's ashen face, he gently moved some hair back from her eyes then he covered them both as best he could with armfuls of hay for warmth. Finally he laid down, exhausted, and slept.

Chapter Thirteen

Both children awoke to the call of a cockerel. It was still dark. Peanut looked around her, pulling hay from her hair. Her clothes were still wet. She felt really uncomfortable and her muscles ached. Bean was also realising just how miserable it was to wake in cold, wet clothes. He was hungry.

Peanut realised that Bean had managed to get her here. She took one look at his face and knew that he was thinking of food. "My bag, it's gone," Peanut croaked in alarm, her tongue was sticking to the roof of her mouth.

"It's here, don't worry," Bean gave the bag to Peanut. "Thanks Bean," she smiled, "I have got some chocolate in here. Just a couple of bars, but we can have one now and one when hunger strikes again later."

The whole world felt a better place to Bean once he was eating, though if they were honest, neither of the children had eaten enough to fill them up. They stood up, shivering and crossed to the door. Looking out they could see it was daybreak.

From somewhere to the left they could hear machines and mooing. "Must be the milking parlour," Bean whispered to Peanut.

He walked a little way forward. They were around the back of a 'U'-shaped farmhouse. To the left of the barn were the cow stalls and milking parlour. To the right lay a huge shed from which emanated herumphing and kicking noises. Must be the bull shed, Bean thought. Further along he could see a large chicken shed and then a barn housing sheep.

The dog barked, he could probably hear them. "The dog must be tied up in the farmyard," Peanut imparted hopefully.

"Let's, go this way," Bean whispered. They went toward the milking parlour where a single lantern was visible in the grey dawning light. Staying very close to the buildings they eventually found an entrance. There seemed to be hundreds of cows inside and the children had literally to push their way through the warm bodies while trying to see, but not be seen.

Eventually as they neared the front of the cattle queue they saw a small and dishevelled girl. She had one arm in a plaster cast and horror of horrors, around her ankle was a huge ball and chain! She was quite literally single handedly milking all these huge animals.

The children stared in amazement. When Peanut could bear it no longer, she moved forward. "Hello, are you Poppy?"

Poppy jumped and turned as swiftly as a ball and chain allows. "Omago, ooo aaah oo?" Poppy asked.

Peanut was a little taken aback; Boris had failed to tell them Poppy wasn't English. She looked back to Bean. He moved forward and shrugged, not knowing which language the girl had spoken.

"Ooo aaah oo?" Poppy tried again. She gave up and signalled writing on paper into the air.

"She wants a pen and paper," Peanut said.

"What use is that if she writes foreign too?"

"She might draw something."
Then to the girl she said, "Boris
sent us. Have we got the right
person, are you Poppy?" Peanut
asked in a loud whisper.

Poppy nodded frantically.

Bean found his empty
chocolate wrapper and a pencil
stub. He passed them to Peanut who

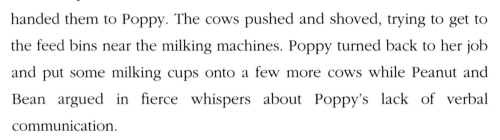

handed them to Poppy. The cows pushed and shoved, trying to get to
the feed bins near the milking machines. Poppy turned back to her job
and put some milking cups onto a few more cows while Peanut and
Bean argued in fierce whispers about Poppy's lack of verbal
communication.

Poppy started to scribble on the paper then she held it out to Peanut.
With really poor writing she had put 'Please help me. They have broken
my arm so I cannot write, tied me to the chain so I cannot escape and
glued my mouth shut so I can't telephone for help.'

"Glued your mouth shut?" Peanut couldn't believe such an archaic
thing could happen in this day and age. "You must come with us
Poppy, we can help you. Escape while you can. We want to try and get
you back to Odd."

"What about the cows? They will suffer if I don't milk them."

"Pants to the cows. If you do help them you will be the one to suffer.
Come on," Bean ordered.

"Your folks will sort them out as soon as they realise you are gone.
It will give them something to do instead of coming after us," Peanut

insisted. She took hold of Poppy's hand and pulled her away. Poppy picked up the ball and carried it in her good arm.

"I'm Peanut, and this is Bean," Peanut said, running away from the milking parlour. They all left through the wooden exit and along the side of the farmhouse towards the road. Peanut had her bag tied inside her coat. It gave added insulation from the cold and kept it safe.

The dog went absolutely ballistic, barking and rattling at its confines. Poppy couldn't run very fast carrying the ball and chain. Then, behind them they heard a gun shot. As one, they dived behind a stack of full bin bags. Bean peered cautiously toward the house.

"Stay thee where you are vermin," bellowed a loud scratchy voice. "I'm coming down, naw then."

"Oh yeah, I'll stay Mr gun-wielding maniac," Bean said with attitude. "NOT!" He grabbed hold of Poppy's ball and chain, "If I carry this, we should be able to run."

They darted towards the hedge by the road, but it was too late. The dog had been released and he had not eaten. He was huge. He overtook the children, then rounded on them, showing his teeth and snarling ferociously. Then he sprang forward and took a huge mouthful of Bean's coat.

They sprang back cowering against the hedge, then a voice said very close to Bean's head, "Gotcha!" A huge, horny, hairy hand took hold of his arm.

Bean turned and looked straight into the barrel of a twelve bore shotgun.

Chapter Fourteen

Poppy was sent back to tend the cows, while Bean and Peanut were escorted past the sheep and into a metal grain store. They felt sick and frightened, positive they would be shot. Each time one of them slowed or stopped the dog would bite their clothing and they felt the gun barrel pushing them in the back. It would be futile to try to escape.

Mr Smashem leered at them, holding his face only inches from theirs. He had huge gaps between his teeth, with bits of black rotting meat stuck in the gaps. The smell of his breath made them recoil. "Pesky vermin, that's what you are. We've got rat poison to deal with the likes of you. Bet thee thought you were so clever, but thou are nothing more than stinking dog turd on my shoes. I can just wipe you off in one go, sithee." He laughed a scratchy laugh, turned and left the grain store. Then with a sinking feeling they heard a key turning in the padlock outside. They were trapped.

"What are we to do now?" Peanut asked as soon as they were sure they were alone. They sat on the floor amidst the dusty grain. They were cold, hungry, tired and fed up. What's more, they had lost Poppy again.

Once the cows were milked, Poppy went on to feed chickens and collect eggs, then fed the bull and sheep. When everything was fed and watered she had to start mucking out all the animal stalls. Her brain was racing. Boris was a dear to send somebody after her. She thought that by now he would have forgotten her.

However much initially she had needed to cling on to hope, when nobody had come she had sadly given in to the belief that nobody was coming. Today she had eaten no breakfast and nothing yet for lunch. Now lunchtime was gone she knew her parents would be taking an afternoon nap.

Poppy sneaked into the kitchen. She had no idea what had happened to the children she had so briefly met. Mr and Mrs Smashem knew Poppy wouldn't steal food, with her mouth glued up she couldn't eat a thing. She collapsed onto a chair, weak with hunger. Every time she had a chance she had been rubbing the glue from her lips, today she had managed to make a tiny gap. It was through this that she pushed breadcrumbs from the table. From the sitting room, deep toned rumbling snores and deeper toned scratchy snores told her that momentarily she was safe, her parents were asleep.

She went to a drawer and took out a straw. She put this into some creamy milk from the fridge and blissfully drank vast quantities of the life-sustaining liquid.

Daring not to stay any longer than necessary, Poppy took a huge chunk of cherry cake from the Welsh dresser, then as quietly as she had entered, she now left the kitchen, pushing the cake into her red dungarees pocket.

Outside, the dog was once again tethered, sleeping in the afternoon sunshine. She went around the back of the house, looking in buildings and sheds as she went. Finally her shoulders slumped as she realised the children were gone. A feeling of dread overcame her. Poppy sat behind a hay bale and started to cry. Her last and only chance of rescue had gone.

Only one building away, Bean and Peanut sat feeling just as dejected. Capture had not been in their plans (or lack of them!) and neither knew what to do next. Not knowing if Mr Smashem was about to return with the poison he had threatened left them jumpy and scared. Bean stood and walked as far around the building as he could get, which wasn't very far because of the mound of grain. He tried the door for the umpteenth time, just in case it wasn't really locked. Then, "I know, we can use a wish!"

Before Peanut had a chance to answer he said, "I wish we were out of here." And they were! Blinking after the darkness of the store, they stood just outside the door.

"Bean you utter idiot," Peanut said, "what about fitting a bit more into the wish, like finding Poppy again?"

"Oim eeer," said Poppy from the other side of the hay bales. Peanut forgot to be angry. They raced around the bales.

Poppy's face lit up when she saw her new friends. Once again Bean took hold of the ball and chain. "Come on, quick." He would have liked to know where Mr Smashem was, but it was a waste of time trying to talk. They raced past the grain store and back across the farmyard where Bean saw a woodpile. He steered the girls into it. There, hanging on the wall, was just what he was looking for: an axe. Slightly rusty and a little blunt, but still an axe!

Grabbing the handle, he draped the chain over the chopping block and hacked at it. The axe was so blunt that the blade just glanced off. He tried again, then again. Peanut kept a watchful eye on the farmhouse. The dog woke and started to bark, making enough racket to wake the dead. Just when they thought it would never break, the chain was cut and the ball rolled a little to one side. Bean threw the axe down, the rusty blade was all dented and bent. "Come on," he said.

They ran toward the road but it was too late. The door was flung open and the Smashems were on their tail. Mrs Smashem was a very strong-looking, sturdy woman. She told them to stay where they were or they would regret it. Bean thought that if they stayed where they were they would regret it even more. He carried on running.

Mr Smashem released the dog, it charged at the children with a great lolloping stride, barking loudly. Soon he was so close that Peanut could feel his breath on her neck. "You two go on ahead," she called, "this dog can't catch all of us." Her knees buckled under her and she fell onto the hard grey road surface.

The dog took one almighty bite at her leg. The pain was incredible. Screaming she saw the other two turn helplessly, not sure if they should run forward or turn back. Bean turned back. Lying there on the road, Peanut felt the all too familiar barrel of Mr Smashem's gun stabbing her in the back. Peanut had had enough.

"I wish we were all three in Thetford, that Poppy's mouth was unstuck and that my leg was healed and pain free," she screamed into the air.

Crash, they landed by the riverside, right in front of a catalogue shop.

"Why Thetford?" Bean asked, puzzled.

"I was so scared, I couldn't think of any other names of places that I knew," she explained apologetically.

"Ow, ooo aargh ow oh that really hurts," Poppy sat up holding her broken arm. "I can speak!" her hand shot up to feel her unglued mouth. Despite the pain in her arm, her face broke into the most enormous grin.

"We've made it, we really have made it!" Peanut was totally overjoyed. "Poppy, consider yourself well and truly rescued. With one wish left, are we cool or what?"

"I'm starving, can we have some of that chocolate you saved Peanut?" Bean rubbed his rumbling tummy.

"I've got some cherry cake too," Poppy offered. They sat for a while, eating and looking at the swans floating along the river. A rusty shopping trolley stuck out of the water at the sort of angle that tells you it wasn't a successful shopping trip. People passed to and fro, some of them even went to other places too.

"Let's use the last wish to get back to Odd," Bean said. They agreed. Taking a last look around, Peanut spotted the face of her father, on the front of a newspaper. "Wait," she cried. She bent down to pick the paper up. 'Bursting Outburst', read the headline. Peanut read the columns below. "He's really gone and done it now," she whispered handing the article to Bean.

He looked at Oliver's photograph and read how the man had simply got so angry that he ate and ate, faster and faster until he exploded. Oliver was no more. They had scraped as much of the man off the dining room walls and door as they could in order to give him a decent burial.

It had shocked Ida so much that she hadn't eaten since. She was quoted as saying, 'When I do eat, it will be healthy food only. Right now I cannot touch a thing. I am going to live with my sister in Australia.'

"I'm sorry. Do you want to keep this, Peanut?" he held the paper up.

Peanut shook her head. "Let's just go. 'We wish we were back in the Land of Odd'."

Chapter Fifteen

The first thing they saw was the upside-down tree. "Poppy, why is the tree upside down?" Peanut asked.

"I'll tell you later," she smiled.

They walked towards the cottage. "We have only been away for two days. It feels like more," Bean said.

"So we are on Myday, we can do as we like. Let's go and find Boris," Poppy suggested.

The cottage kitchen door stood slightly ajar, but Boris wasn't there. The children had a drink of water; they were all very thirsty. Bean had only managed to get a drink at the train station, though Peanut had a drink of water at home and at the station. They went out into the garden and around to the shed. Still no sign of Boris.

The sunshine was very hot so they decided to leave their coats in the kitchen and walk to the river. If Boris returned he would know they were back. Along the path they met many different creatures that recognised and greeted them. Poppy pointed out her tree house and a little den. She mentioned how much she missed Boris and Mrs Batty, but particularly Boots. "He has a very dry sense of humour. If you listen to the one or two things he says, it is like watching a comedy. Mrs Batty is very serious and doesn't realise he is pulling her leg," she told them.

"He was quite polite when we went last week to fix the roof," Peanut told her. She bent down and picked up a new Super-Zapper. A little further along Bean found one too.

The river was still a five-minute walk away, but already they could hear the happy voices. They sped up to join in and there in the clearing an amazing sight met their eyes. Children of many races and many descriptions surrounded an old gentleman. As they got closer they could hear him telling a story. Every time he forgot to keep his arms still, a frog or some other creature would fall, seemingly from out of nowhere and land amidst the group who would scream or duck and move away altogether.

Some children were using umbrellas for safety, but others were sitting in the water a safer distance away. Obviously they were aware that elephants were included in the prevailing creature-falling conditions.

Each time Boris got to a funny part of his story, all the children fell about laughing. When it was scary they all oohed and aahed. When Bean could contain himself no longer, he lifted the Super-Zapper and took aim. Peanut grinned and did the same. Poppy said, "You wouldn't, would you?"

"We would," they chorused and fired the Zappers straight at Boris. Zing, Zing. Splut, splut. Two enormous yellow stars flew through the air. Boris looked up as the stars hit him, one on the forehead, the other on his shoulder. His mouth opened, slowly he stood up. By now everybody had turned to see who had fired them. Silence surrounded the riverbank. You could have heard an ant cough.

"Poppy?" he whispered. Then louder, "Poppy, is it really you?" He started to walk toward the straggly, sickly looking child with her broken arm. Everybody cleared a pathway for his first stumbling steps. Tears filled his eyes. "Oh my, oh Poppy, it really is you!" He reached down and scooped her up in his arms. "It really is MYDAY," he shouted to everybody. Whistles and claps filled the air. Then Boris noticed Peanut and Bean standing there, grinning like loonies. "My children, all together and safe at last. I owe you both, big time!"

People crowded around asking questions and shaking their hands. Neither Peanut nor Bean knew what to say or answer first.

"I knew you had achieved a great deal when children started to arrive on Funday, then today more and more came, but you didn't. I was so worried, now here you are." Boris wiped his eyes. "Well, you got me good and proper with the Zappers; the least I can do is offer you tea!" His eyes shone, and his arms remained firmly around Poppy. "Let's go back to the cottage, you must be worn out." He turned and waved to everybody, then they were going back along the path.

"All the children who have arrived so far have been housed by people already here. Now all we will be doing on Theirday is to help each other build extensions for extra children. In Odd it is considered to be a great honour to get chosen by a child to provide a place for them to live. We put a lot of effort into it. Mrs Batty has put in a request for assistance in building two extra rooms. She hopes that for a while she and I can share you, Poppy." Boris looked fondly down at Poppy. "Perhaps once your arm is mended you might like to go and stay with her. That will give her time to get the extension built."

He looked at Bean and Peanut. "You are both very brave children, I'm not just grateful to you, I am proud of you." Embarrassed, they looked down at their feet walking along the path. Bean's shoes were covered in mud, his trousers had dog's mouth-sized tears in them and his shirt hung limply, creased and dirty.

Shortly, a pony and trap came along to give them all a lift. They thanked the pony for his thoughtfulness. Peanut lay down as they

jogged along. Exhausted, she watched the sky through the branches and leaves. She knew she was on her way home. She felt grimy. They hadn't been able to brush their teeth or wash or change their clothes. Hers, too, were torn and dishevelled.

Bean lounged against the side of the cart. Poppy nestled up to Boris, who told her they would soon have her right in no time. The hooves clip-clopped along the pathway. The only other sound was an uproarious singing from all the birds, as they passed the news from nest to nest. The 'Hero Children' had returned!

Back in the kitchen, Boris made them all tea, manually! Peanut said "I have something for you." She emptied the bag into a pile on the table. "May I take your cloak, Boris? I can sew while you are doing our tea."

"You got them, excellent. You are a clever girl. So many remnants too, you must have cursed their weight on your journey." It hadn't actually occurred to her to do that. Why would she when they were so desperately needed and she could help? Peanut smiled. She felt very content.

Boris told her there would be plenty of time to sew once they had washed, changed, had eaten and were rested. He told them to go and look at their rooms. The children raced up the stairs. Peanut stopped at the door as she realised that she had only been borrowing Poppy's room. She let Poppy go forward to open the door.

Inside there was only a little dressing room. The bedroom had vanished. Peanut looked in startled. In front of the girls were two doors. Poppy's name was on one. On the other it said 'Peanut'. Each girl went into her new room and were both really glad to find it hadn't changed at all! Boris had got all his friends to build an extension, then dress both rooms alike so both girls could feel at home immediately.

When Bean got to his door he was very proud to see his name on it. It truly felt like home. The girls agreed.

Back in the kitchen Boris told them they could make any changes to their rooms that they chose as and when it suited them. They sat down wearily to an amazing spread of delicious food, telling Boris, in between mouthfuls, of their adventures.

When Peanut came to the part about her father's sad demise her voice wavered then petered out all together. A lump sat in her throat, she couldn't go on without bursting into tears so she just sat and hung her head. The loyal child, after all Oliver had put her through, she had still loved him. He was her father.

Bean took over and explained to Boris. His face was very grave as he cast his eyes over the poor girl. "So you'll be needing a more permanent home then, won't you, Peanut?"

Peanut nodded. "If that's okay Boris, may I stay here?" she asked quietly.

"I thought I told you little one, I owe you an enormous debt. My home is your home. Here you can just be you. So that is one broken arm and one broken heart we shall be mending." He smiled gently at Peanut. She smiled back.

"Can you find room for a permanent home for me too?" Bean asked. "Only I didn't go home and to be honest I don't want to."

"Of course." Then to all three children he said, "Welcome home. Come on tuck in, there is plenty more if you need it." Bean didn't need telling twice, he was ravenous.

Suddenly, through the open door, came a bright pink star followed by a fluorescent green moon. They hit Boris on the shoulder. "I think we have company," he said going to the doorway. Shortly triplet boys joined them. Henry, Steven and Harry. They grinned sheepishly but were very happy to join in the meal.

Chatting away they found they all had so much in common. Soon two girls joined them, Daisy and Molly.

"Odd is getting to be a very popular resort," laughed Boris.

"Party!" exclaimed Bean with his mouth momentarily empty.

After a bath that evening, Peanut insisted on making a start on Boris's Cloak. She felt that it would be needed quicker than ever with the amount of visitors they were getting. Boris admitted it made sense to be able to magic food and accommodation. Manual work would take too long.

Boris sat down too and started on the other end. "I love the patterns on this material," he said holding up a piece with blue and green swirls on, "It is just like peacock feathers."

The four boys were playing a game of cards and Poppy was fast asleep in a rocking chair by the fire. The other two girls had left to go

back to their new home with a neighbour called Mrs Lambin. She had
been utterly delighted, and to think she had only called in to see if the
children had returned safely and bring news of Ma and Pa Baddle.

The entire kitchen was bathed in a homely glowing light.

Suddenly Peanut remembered something. "Poppy, you were going
to tell us why that tree is upside
down."

Poppy grinned. "You tell
them, Boris."

"The tree is upside down
because that's just Odd!" he
answered simply. Then they all
fell about laughing.

The End.

The prices shown below were correct at the time of going to press. However, Taverner Publications reserve the right to show new retail prices on covers which may differ from those previously advertised in the text or elsewhere.

Please supply .... copies of *Zap the Wizard and the Land of Odd,* at £3.99 per book (plus postage and packing).

Please make cheques made payable to G. Wilkinson, and send to:

Taverner Publications, Taverner House, Harling Road, East Harling, Norfolk NR16 2QR

Postage and Packing:

UK and BFPO customers please send a cheque or postal order (no currency) and allow one pound for postage and packing for the first book plus 50p for each additional book.

Overseas customers, including Eire, please allow two pounds for postage and packing of the first book plus one pound for each additional book ordered.

Please complete in BLOCK CAPITALS

NAME ....

ADDRESS ....

....

.... POSTCODE ....

I have enclosed cheque or postal order number ....

for the amount of £ .... sterling.